DON'T EAT THE SANDWICHES!

HOWARD G AWBERY

Published by New Generation Publishing in 2019

Cover illustration by Sammy Johnson.

ISBN: 978-1-78955-851-7

www.newgeneration-publishing.com

New Generation Publishing

For Jane

Once life was all about need, now it's all about greed.

1

Veronica pushed down with all her weight on the bulging, brown, borrowed suitcase. One slightly rusty clasp had locked shut, the other definitely had not.

Scanning the enormous pile of already jettisoned holiday clothes strewn across the bed, there wasn't anything else she could possibly leave out. Veronica knew she should have packed sooner, and the guilty fact irritated her.

Sweating, she heaved her not inconsiderable weight above the offending clasp and launched herself at the target. The two parts moved slightly closer together. Another bounce should do it; only a quarter of an inch to go and the second clasp would click shut. She could then start her holiday with a vengeance courtesy of the large bottle of Asti Spumante chilling in the fridge.

Every now and again Veronica employed her sensible head for decisions and right now it was in a quandary. Should she continue bouncing on the last quarter of an inch to shut the remaining clasp, risking the borrowed suitcase bursting in the taxi on the way to the airport or, even worse, exploding at the Spanish airport baggage reclaim? She winced at the thought of turning puce with embarrassment, weaving between holidaymakers, trying to keep up with the baggage carousel as she snatched her clothes off one by one, stuffing them into anything she was able to find.

Or would she laugh along with everyone else at somebody's misfortune until everyone had collected their luggage and then, when there was nobody around, furtively collect the tatters of her holiday wardrobe and ragged suitcase? On the other hand, her sensible head was gently suggesting she should empty the suitcase and carefully repack it, leaving out even more clothes.

Veronica knew the root cause of the suitcase dilemma was not having lost the weight she'd faithfully promised herself she would lose four months ago. Then, she had vowed she would leave twenty pounds of ugly fat in England before she boarded the big, silver bird on her way to paradise (or two weeks in Spain). She had visualised herself travelling in a loose, flowery, size twelve summer dress. Her clothes would only be half the volume, allowing her to pack twice as many, and she would feel like a million dollars every day.

Life for Veronica was never that simple and her ambitious plans had gone awry. Four months previously, she had pledged to herself that today she would be packing pretty silk kanga, flimsy pants with less material than she used to floss her teeth, and size 36C lacy bras.

However, what she had actually set aside to travel in was a bell-tent denim dress that could sleep a full scout troop if pegged out and, instead of flimsy underwear, her everyday enormous pants that were ten times as big and heavy as the ones she had dreamed of slipping into. Her swimming costume wouldn't look any worse on a 45 gallon oil drum despite being described in the lying brochure as slimming black, and her selection of bras could be used to haul concrete up a multi-storey building site!

How she envied her cousin Joanne who always dressed as if she was about to meet the love of her life, and had such a biology-defying small waist that Veronica often wondered how her organs managed to fit inside her.

Joanne had been blessed with a metabolism that burnt everything she consumed, whereas Veronica was cursed with a more frugal metabolism that stored half of everything she consumed. What sane man would choose her when sylph-like Joanne was parading next to her in Malaga? Joanne would be sitting on a nightclub stool sporting a tight, skimpy dress held up by spider's web straps that exaggerated her petite figure. She, on the other hand, would be sporting an end-of-season, final reduction empire style dress looking like Joanne's minder.

However, Veronica was an optimist and there was always hope. Once Joanne had fixed herself up with the best-looking man around, Veronica believed she would be in with a chance with the second best-looking man, or maybe even third, but at least she would be in with a chance as the evenings lengthened.

She was well aware that excessive alcohol distorted male vision, and the trick was to make sure she pulled when the male in question was only three quarters of the way down the alcohol spiral. If lucky, any conquest would still be reasonably coherent, would buy her drinks, could walk unaided and, if called upon, could perform adequately before ultimately finding his own way home.

Snapping out of her daydream and returning to her

packing, Veronica was confident that Joanne would be travelling with her matching set of suitcases, full of skimpy bikinis and silk blouses layered in ultra-neat tissue. Her packing would have been planned and executed a fortnight ago, at least! Enough thinking. Decision impetuously made!

With a final leap, Veronica launched herself onto the truculent, grinning, open corner of the suitcase. Unfortunately, before she could close the clasp, the defiant suitcase slid off the end of the bed with Veronica riding bareback.

Crashing onto the bedroom floor on its open corner, followed by Veronica landing on the opposite corner, the ageing suitcase exploded, scattering its entire contents across the bedroom floor.

"S***. S***. S***." Veronica looked around; her bedroom now looked like the end of a Boxing Day sale.

"Last bloody minute again," she chided herself as she wiped perspiration-wet hair from her forehead.

Struggling to rise off the floor, she kicked in temper at the muddle of clothes on her way out of the bedroom and powered towards the kitchen fridge. There she poured herself a very large glass of chilled holiday fizz. The original bottle, positioned in the fridge door four months ago as a weight loss incentive only to be opened the night before her holiday, had already been swapped many times. The bottle had been replaced following every minor disaster in her life, especially after her weekly weigh-in at Trim Club.

Veronica tore at the top of a jumbo pack of cheese and onion crisps as a special treat. They smelled so good as she ripped at the greasy bag; the cheese was Gorgonzola and the red onions made her eyes water. The onion fire was quickly quenched by the wine and the sharpness of the cheese bit at her lips. “Wonderful.”

Tonight she was, once again, on her own so could eat what she liked. In Malaga she would need to be more cautious, for the worst thing to choose from the Spanish menu would be a plateful of local sausage laced with enough garlic to light a candle at ten yards. That would definitely put off any possible suitor. As would eating a large portion of duvet lifting Jerusalem artichokes before snuggling up to her handsome, fantasy, Spanish beau.

Slumping down on the wheezing sofa like a well-fed cat, she flicked through her ticket, her passport and the holiday itinerary. It looked amazing. Two weeks of hot sunshine. No alarm clock, no bloody weigh-ins, no work, no bosses, no exercise, and no walking. Nothing. Just sand, sea, fizz and bronzed Spaniards with flashing eyes and long, shiny, black hair.

Flakes of crisps fluttered onto her jeans and she brushed them off nonchalantly, excusing the action by announcing out loud to the furniture in her cramped flat, “I am now officially on holiday!”

The day after her decision to go on holiday with Joanne, and being anxious about two weeks of comparison whilst away, Veronica had joined a gym, gone on a diet, started walking to work, given up alcohol, given up crisps and even given up fags.

The following day, however, she had re-declared her weight reduction vow to herself, and again the following day, and again the following day. She had tried to lose weight, she really had, but it was all such a chore and thin folk just didn’t understand the plight of big-boned people. A slow metabolism was the problem and she couldn't change that, could she?

It was genetic. It was her mother's fault entirely, she reflected. It wasn't even as if her mother was a good cook but what she missed out on with quality, she counteracted with quantity. Even her mild natured father referred to her mother as a graduate of the karate school of cooking – "She could kill you with just one chop!" – but, on the positive side, he had to admit she had cured the dog of begging.

Veronica deduced her mother must have had big family genes coupled with a slow metabolism, and her gran on her mother's side must have had enormous genes. Her gran's philosophy on appearance was that she should keep eating until all of her wrinkles were filled out! So, it was not surprising Veronica struggled with her weight. In fact, she felt she was doing rather well compared with the two of them.

Her on and off life of diets had oscillated faster than an excited Labrador puppy's tail. She had tried fasting for three days a week, a banana diet, a seaweed-ten-times-a-day diet, a no carbs diet, an only carbs diet, a just meat diet and a no meat diet. The list went on and on.

Veronica's foray into the world of weight loss clubs had not ended well either. She chose not to join fat clubs or boot camps, but rather liked the concept of Trim Club. It had seemed more dignified and she had reasoned there was plenty of time to lose the weight at a leisurely rate before her holiday. Twenty pounds to get off? Easy!

Weekly, she stood in line with all the other Trim Club members at the obligatory weigh-in; everyone respectful of the imaginary privacy line, one yard back from the current member being weighed. The conversation between the member being weighed and the person recording the weight was always in discreet, hushed tones, avoiding any possible chance of embarrassment.

In week three Veronica hadn't eaten or drunk anything, squeezing every last drop of fluid out in a big wee whilst wearing her thinnest top and lightest trousers. She had considered not wearing any underwear, but decided to leave that ploy in case she had a really bad week in the future. Soon it was her turn: shoes off, bag down, purse down, watch off, rings off, handkerchief out and keys on the table. She stepped onto the scales and stood ramrod still, not wanting to jog the needle upwards, and waited for the result.

"Veronica, my dear, you have popped on five pounds this week. Any thoughts?" whispered the ever-enthusiastic Trim Club weigher.

Veronica snatched her book back and gathered up her shoes, bag, purse, watch, rings, handkerchief and keys. She had plenty of thoughts. After all the secrecy at the front of the line, Veronica then had to run the gauntlet of all the other women asking loudly how she had done.

"Well?"

"Well what?" she snapped back as she walked past the enquiring line, her eyes belying their incendiary potential.

"How did you get on this week?" asked a lady wearing a man's T-shirt and a pair of leggings two sizes too small with all the stitching stretched beyond its safe limit.

"Five pounds."

"On or off?"

"On," snapped Veronica.

"Who's been a naughty girl then?" chimed in the only man in the queue as if talking to a child. He was wearing an open necked shirt and jeans with buttons so stretched at the fly that if one flew off Veronica thought it would kill someone.

"Who's been visiting the kebab van then?" joked another half way down.

"Remember, little pickers wear bigger knickers, and bigger pickers wear even bigger knickers," the last lady in the queue ordeal added.

Veronica's lop-sided, embarrassed smile only partially hid her whispered reply to the queue. "P*** off."

The final indignity was still to come in Trim Club's plenary wrap up session. Following the obligatory deep-breathing exercise, when everyone was saying a quiet, "Thank God that's over for another week!" it was encouraged to applaud the member who had lost the most weight. In total, the class had lost nearly two stones.

"It would have been over two stones - a class record for a week and a big bonus for me," the leader lamented, "except for one lady who put on everything that seven other members had lost!"

Veronica decided there and then she didn't need the embarrassment of a ritual Friday ridiculing, she could lose the weight on her own and it would be considerably cheaper.

The lead up to her holiday in her job at a retail distribution warehouse had not included her finest hour either. When she excitedly announced she was so looking forward to her holiday, the comment was met with some bewilderment. Her confused boss pulled her into his office and asked when she was going, to be told by Veronica that her flight was early the next day - Saturday morning at 4.00 am. She went on to explain that they hadn't been able to book a later flight for a number of reasons. All this was lost on her boss and he looked very puzzled.

"But Veronica, you haven't booked the time off. Dave and Maggie are off from tomorrow for two weeks. They both booked it weeks ago. The three of you can't be off at the same time; there'll be nobody to manage the warehouse."

"I booked the holiday when I put the leave slip on your desk and, what's more, you signed it. Here it is, you bozo." And with that, in triumph, from her cavernous filing cabinet handbag filled with old receipts, empty crisp packets and unopened bills, she miraculously produced the crumpled, grubby slip, dutifully signed by her boss.

"There see, old age doesn't come alone does it, you poor soul? You must have forgotten you signed it before you signed theirs, so I'm off to sunny Spain in the morning for two glorious weeks!"

Her boss pored over the crumpled sheet and announced, "But this is for two weeks starting on Saturday 15th August 1975. Next month! We're in July now, the seventh month, not the eighth month that you wrote down. See, you wrote 15/8/1975." He showed Veronica the paper. "The eighth month is August. I'm sorry, but you'll just have to cancel your holiday and go when you originally booked the time off in August. You can't all be off at the same time."

He was right. It was Veronica's mistake. She had entered the wrong month. She winced, she swore under her breath and then declared, "Tough! I've worked for this holiday, I've saved for this holiday and I've even lost bloody weight for this holiday, although not much I'll grant you. Tomorrow I'll be on a beach with an ice-cold Pina Colada in one hand and a Spaniard in the other. If you think I'll be in on Monday you're in fairy land!"

With that, she flicked her bag onto her shoulder and marched off. Just as she was leaving his office she started to sing, "Viva Espana".

"Well, don't come back in two weeks!" shouted the boss.

His comment only made Veronica sing even louder.

Right then, at that precise moment, all the job pain and weight loss failure was well and truly behind her. As she sat on the sofa with her fizz and crisps she determined she was going to enjoy her holiday no matter what! Big people are happy people, she had read somewhere, and on this holiday she was going to be really, really happy.

2

Passport

Tickets

Money

Sun cream

After sun

Glasses

Medicines

Adaptors

Joanne's previous summer holiday's list served as a good guide for her forthcoming holiday. Forgotten items had been dutifully added following the detailed post-mortem, and unnecessary items had been ejected.

In fact, she had two lists - one for her main suitcase and one for her hand luggage. The hand luggage took as much careful planning as the full-sized luggage, having once arrived at Malaga airport while her baggage was landing at exactly the same time at Madrid airport! Despite being in the same country, they weren't reunited until the last day of her holiday. Joanne's worst nightmare!

When Joanne was immersed in details about planning, cost processes and best value for money, she was in her element. Lists, forms, inventories, balance sheets, cost-benefit-analysis exercises, cash flow statements and expense forms were her whole life, and what gave her joy.

Her career and life were grounded in tidiness and attention to detail. In her precise ecosphere she was absolutely content, and she had been rewarded early on by a series of plum accountancy practice jobs after leaving school. The career ladder had been quickly ascended and, until recently, she held a position of some status and very respectable remuneration.

However, she reflected that her penchant for order had also been the cause of the breakdown of her first marriage to a good looking guy called Keith. Endless lists and attention to detail had been just too much for a normal, untidy young guy. Keith didn't need his socks pairing or his pants ironing, folding, co-ordinating and all facing the same way, in the same colour sequence, in the very same drawer every Wednesday. He hated any level of order and routine.

Keith loved what Joanne referred to as his abjectly chaotic life. He was happy with his excessively elevated tolerance of disorder, his juvenile untidiness, and his complete disregard for time. Keith never wore a suit, claiming it restricted where he could comfortably be with his friends, like a bar. He never wore his watch, declaring he'd lost the hour hand some years ago, but would get it fixed one day. He never polished his shoes, believing only accountants had time to polish their shoes. Keith preferred to wear loose jeans, a faded T-shirt, and trainers that didn't have laces. He merged perfectly into the world of computer programming where the dress code was jumble sale.

He yearned for confusion, excitement, impulsiveness, freedom and spontaneity in his life. Keith wanted a wife who, on an impulse, would be happy to jump in the car with him on a Friday evening and not know, nor care, where they were headed; a complete anathema for Joanne. She admitted the sex had been good but the price had been just too high. They parted two years after their marriage.

Joanne's second husband, Gordon Wendover, had been 20 years her senior. She had done juvenile with Keith, and Gordon was mature, settled and steady. On their dates he was the epitome of courtesy and respect: always on time and accompanied by a bunch of flowers or box of chocolates. Such a wonderful opposite to Keith. Gordon was a dependable gentleman with what could best be described as a grandfatherly disposition. In Gordon, she at last found order, cleanliness, neatness, processes and impeccable timekeeping; such a breath of fresh air, such a find.

However, so set in his ways was he that even Joanne, with her passion for routine and detail, became rapidly irked.

For instance, who has the identical first meal of the day at 7.00 am on the dot every day, weekday and weekends, even Christmas Day? Who has the same breakfast of weighed out cornflakes with measured out almond milk, heated to just below boiling for three minutes? This had to be followed immediately by toast.

And how on earth can anyone get toast wrong? But initially, get it wrong she did. Gordon's toast needed to be served buttered, piping hot and one slice at a time. Floppy toast just wasn't toast at all to him; it was warm, limp, brown bread! For the first six months of their marriage the kitchen smoke detector regularly accompanied their breakfast conversation, until Joanne mastered the petulant foibles of the machine. Eventually, his toast was served, to his delight, prepared to perfection.

Accompanying the precise timing of the meals, Joanne's dining room table had to be laid with all the accoutrements of yesteryear; a veritable antique shop of eating tools.

"Who still uses a toast rack?" she would grumble. "Who still uses a teapot, tea cosy and tea strainer, or museum marmalade spoons, or silver sugar tongs for lump sugar?" she would whinge. "Who still uses a napkin and silver serviette ring?" she would ask herself. "What family in England still has a cruet set including freshly prepared mustard every day, complete with a doll's house silver mustard spoon?" she would grouse.

To be fair, Gordon didn't necessarily want her to prepare breakfast for him, or lay the table for him, but if she didn't do it he took hours over what to her had always been the fastest meal of the day. In her more guilty moments she had an inclination of what her first husband had suffered.

Sadly, Gordon died an untimely death in the bath. One Saturday evening at 7.00 pm precisely, accompanied by two fingers of malt whisky and five lavender candles of differing heights burning in the bathroom, whilst listening to Vivaldi's Four Seasons, he suffered a heart attack and died instantly. Saturday evening had always been his bath night.

Depending on how one views Providence, on this occasion it did help to extricate Joanne from the trying ordeal with Gordon.

After the initial shock of her husband's death, Joanne's emotional armour had been dented but not penetrated. Soon, her mercenary side started to surface and she secretly began to look forward to being left comfortably off. However, it was not to be. All his declared financial wealth had been willed to his children, which they had made very sure of before their father was allowed to wed a 'bimbo', as they had referred to their new, young stepmother.

He had not excluded Joanne completely from his will. Generously, in his eyes, he had bequeathed her his irritable ginger cat called Humphrey. Humphrey had become a major contributor to the vet's pension scheme on account of his regular and noisy fur ball discharges, which were always followed by ghastly explosions of flatulence. Apparently, daily medication was essential.

Gordon also willed Joanne his precious, but aged, Jaguar 2.4 car that had recently failed its MOT with terminal afflictions. Finally, he left her his declining business in the form of a tired funeral parlour. Gordon's poetic solicitor described the business as, "An exciting business opportunity awaiting an injection of youth, energy and enthusiasm."

The willed funeral parlour was housed in a large, detached building situated half way down a quiet cul-de-sac, just off the high street. Over time, both sides of the funeral parlour had been in-filled with terraced houses. These houses had been built where the stables and paddock had once housed the four magnificent black horses that pulled an ornate, glass covered hearse.

On the opposite side of the road was a continuous row of identical terraced houses, only differentiated by the colours of their front doors. Alongside the relatively grand, double fronted funeral parlour, stood a wooden, barn-sized entrance to the garage of the present day motorised hearse.

The funeral parlour was managed by Vincent, an elderly gentleman, and his wife Elsie. Vincent, like Joanne's husband Gordon, was endowed with a most respectful countenance - a necessary behaviour of the profession, Joanne acknowledged.

Early on in her ownership of the funeral parlour Joanne decided to allow Vincent and Elsie to manage the unsavoury business. Between them, they accomplished whatever was required to run everything smoothly. Joanne decided she would stay in the financial sector and have nothing to do with the death sector, except for collecting a steady stream of cash at the end of every month.

As the early months of her ownership rolled by, Joanne realised the word "miracle" was the descriptor omitted from the "exciting business opportunity awaiting an injection of youth, energy and enthusiasm" as the steady stream of cash reduced to a trickle.

Whenever she tackled Vincent about the diminishing performance of the business all he would say was, "We need a harsh winter, a good flu epidemic, or a cholera or diphtheria outbreak like in the old days. Those would shepherd the guests in. In this profession, while there's death there's always hope, my dear. While there's death there's always hope, as Mr Gordon Wendover used to say."

Joanne sighed heavily, as she always did whenever she thought of the funeral parlour, but she decided there was nothing more she could do before her holiday and she so needed a break. But even her holiday was not going to be the holiday she needed.

Somehow, she was once again going on holiday with her cousin Veronica. How had that happened? She had vowed to herself never, ever again to go on holiday with Veronica after the fiasco of their final party night on their last holiday. After the homeward journey, Joanne remembered she had needed wheelchair assistance through the airports, and her leg still gave her gip in frosty weather.

Yet the irrevocable decision to go on holiday together again had been made. It had been made at one of Veronica's impromptu parties where rowdy music and flaming Sambuca shots ensured, by the end of the night, anything was possible and anyone was everyone's friend. There was no going back on the decision now so she would just have to tolerate Veronica and make the most of it.

However, another ghastly thought suddenly entered her mind - she and Veronica were sharing! Single occupancy hotel rooms came at too high a price for her and life hadn't been altogether kind to Joanne recently. If she wanted a holiday, certain sacrifices needed to be made. Sharing with Veronica was one of those sacrifices.

Joanne's ill fortune commenced about six months ago, soon after she lost Gordon. Up until then she had been in a job to die for. She had been a middle manager in the highly reputed accountancy firm of Fox, Fox and Squance Ltd. for two years.

That job came to an abrupt end when, at 2.00 pm one sleepy Friday afternoon, a whole posse of tax investigators burst into their offices waving their badges and telling everyone to stand up and not touch their ledgers. Everything, absolutely everything, was boxed up and taken away. The staff were even asked to empty their handbags and coat pockets.

Apparently, the most senior partner and major shareholder, Mr Percy Fox, had been defrauding the tax office for some years and that Friday was retribution day. In handcuffs, he was led way. Five days later, the ledgers were returned and life temporarily resumed without Mr Percy Fox, at the newly named firm of Fox and Squance Ltd.

One week later Albert Fox, Percy's elder brother, suddenly decided he no longer had any appetite for the business of Fox and Squance Ltd. and its tarnished reputation, and departed for an extended Barbados vacation in an uncharacteristic hurry.

The third partner, Desmond Squance, whose poor health was now in free-fall following the recent events, was left to wind up the company. One month after Albert Fox's disappearance Desmond chose, without consultation or warning, to shut the office of the recently renamed Squance Ltd.

He informed all their clients that Squance Ltd. was ceasing to trade as of the following Monday morning when all documents belonging to clients would be returned. Staff were all paid in lieu of notice and a for sale notice adorned the outside of the building.

Joanne was spitting tacks because in the few months she had been at the company as a young widow, she had been hatching a plan to secure her future. Who did Joanne have in her cross-hairs? Yes, the highly eligible, major shareholder, Percy Fox. By far the most business savvy (despite an aversion to paying tax), by far the richest, and by far the brightest and smartest dressed of the three partners. He was also by far the best looking with his chocolate drop, come to bed eyes, gym trim physique and single status.

She had finally been invited to join him, on her own, for an early evening drink after work on the exact day of the raid. The timing could not have been worse. Her drinks tête-à-tête never happened, her fling never happened, and her future security for life disappeared in handcuffs.

Where was Percy now? Languishing at Her Majesty's Pleasure. All that flirting, all those innuendos, all those nights working late, and all those costly dresses to arouse Percy had been for nought. What a waste. What a cost. What a lesson!

3

One Friday evening, before their cocoa, Christopher and Rosie Gilliam leaned their matching new cases against the wall in their magnolia hallway, alongside their matching new in-flight rucksacks. Draped over their cases were matching walking jackets, and beside each case was a pair of lightweight walking boots, matching and new of course!

The row of holiday luggage was overseen by three white pot ducks ascending in size and flying in formation on the wall towards the front door, symbolising that this was to be their first holiday starting with an aeroplane flight.

Their three bed end of terrace was pristine in appearance, with its manicured lawn and carefully pruned roses, ready for their summer holiday. The drive had been meticulously swept, and the pea gravel around the house raked flat. All in preparation for a two week absence of the occupants.

Arrangements had been made with a kindly neighbour for their curtains to be pulled every night and morning, and for the lights to be turned on and off at irregular intervals. The bin was loaded with rubbish for the first week, and a sack was ready in the garage with saved rubbish for the second week. Letters and parcels would be snatched off the postman and placed out of sight inside the vacated house. Milk would be delivered as normal and used by the kindly neighbour, then the empties would be placed back on their doorstep.

To the casual and even the more determined observer the house gave the appearance of being fully occupied, such were Christopher's preparations.

The Gilliams' long awaited summer holiday had eventually arrived. They were content in the knowledge that the little hardware shop they owned and both worked in was being safely looked after by Rosie's brother and his wife.

Everything possible had been planned to take the stress off their temporary staff too. Suppliers of nails, paint and kitchenware had all been briefed not to call for two weeks while they were away. Suppliers of bird seed and rabbit straw had been instructed by Christopher to deliver enough stock for three weeks. So it went on and on - nothing was being left to chance by Christopher in their little hardware shop.

The following day, their summer holiday would begin with their first ever plane flight. Saturday was to be their thirtieth wedding anniversary, so they had decided to push the boat out. They were so excited that both of them had trouble sleeping.

4.00 am eventually came and they hopped out of bed on the first ring of the Smith's double bell, early bird alarm clock. Being their first plane flight and their first sortie abroad, they had asked advice from friends. All that came back was, “It’s easy, just go with the flow, relax and enjoy yourselves.”

The taxi toot-tooted at 4.50 am and they were outside in a shot, not wanting to disturb the neighbours further. Rosie giggled when the driver asked, “Where to, guv?”

Christopher very assertively said, “The airport - terminal two please, driver.” He squeezed her arm affectionately and she squeezed his back.

At the airport they were driven right to the departures entrance and the taxi driver, being an understanding soul and it being evident it was his passengers’ first time at any airport, went inside and directed them to the correct check-in desk for Spain.

After queuing for about half an hour, they arrived at the check-in desk and Christopher gave the booking lady the name of their Spanish hotel, the street, the town, and eventually the name of the destination Spanish airport.

The booking lady smiled at their newness and wished all passengers were as polite and excited as these two. As their matching luggage disappeared on a conveyor belt Christopher asked if he would have to get his own luggage off the plane at the other end.

“No, Sir, your luggage will be taken off the plane by the ground crew in Spain at Malaga airport. It will be placed on a carousel where you can collect it before you go through customs. I hope you both have a lovely holiday.”

“Thank you,” he beamed gratefully before whispering to Rosie, “What a lovely lady.”

“Yes, wasn’t she,” Rosie agreed.

At this point both Rosie and Christopher had calmed. They were at the airport on time and were now booked onto the flight and had their boarding passes. Each was looking forward to relaxing with a cup of tea and maybe some toast whilst they waited for take-off. There was nothing to fear as they approached security for neither had anything to be concerned about in what they were carrying.

The security process, however, was a nightmare. Immediately behind them was a well-oiled stag party of seasoned travellers, who had already breakfasted in the Irish bar on beer and cigarettes and couldn't understand why everything had to be explained to the first time flyers several times over.

Once they were through security, the now fraught couple hurried to the departure gate already exhausted by the stress of the ordeal.

An announcement over the Tannoy system informing them of a late change of gate to the other side of the airport was the last straw for Christopher. If he mentioned it once, he mentioned it a hundred times to Rosie. "There was never any of this palaver as we crossed from Devon into Cornwall in our camper van". He added, "You do know we'll have to go through this whole rigmarole again in reverse. You do realise that, don't you?"

Eventually, they found their seats on the plane and settled ready for take-off. Rosie turned to Christopher and said, "You know I love you very much, don't you?"

"What brought that on?" asked Christopher, a bit taken aback.

"Well, only the other day I was reading a magazine in the

hairdresser's that said the most dangerous time on any flight is the first twenty seconds after take-off."

"Thank you, Rosie," Christopher answered sarcastically. "That's not the best piece of reassurance I needed on my maiden flight." After a few seconds he relented. "You know I love you too."

They held hands until the plane was in the air and their first time view out of the windows was so fantastic that their minds were taken off the twenty second take-off myth. The next ten minutes were spent trying to identify buildings and roads on the ground. When they flew over their house they told everyone sitting close by, including the air hostess who smiled at the excitement of the first time flyers.

The drinks trolley was soon on its travels and the noisy stag party kept it busy for quite a while.

Shortly after came the trolley with the hot food, and the air hostess asked if the couple wanted the chicken or vegetarian meal. They politely refused both options.

A few seconds later the air hostess returned and asked the same question, "Chicken or vegetarian?" Yet she received the very same reaction - both thanking her, but politely refusing.

A third attempt by the very pleasant, but persistent, air hostess was finally met with an explanation from Rosie. "Thank you, dear, but we've only booked self-catering."

4

The taxi was late, the traffic lights were against them at every crossroad, and the taxi was unable to park anywhere near the departure lounge.

As Joanne and Veronica eventually bustled in through the doors, their first task was to find the departures board. There it was: Malaga, gate 21, on time, check-in desk 12. They joined the queue which seemed surprisingly short, but it was a cruel illusion. It snaked backwards and forwards in front of the check-in desk, making travellers dizzy even before take-off.

"We'll be here all day. There's only one person on the desk. I bet we miss our flight," snapped Joanne as she tried to count the number of people in the queue in front of them.

"We won't miss the flight," reassured Veronica. "If we do, then loads of these people will too."

"Oh, it makes me feel a lot better that we won't be the only ones to miss the flight. By the way please tell me you've got your passport."

"Check, Jo Jo."

"And is it valid for more than three months after our return journey? You did check, didn't you?"

"Err, err, yes, of course I did, Jo Jo," said Veronica nervously with her fingers crossed.

There was a pause while Veronica tried to calculate the weeks left on her well-thumbed passport.

"Here, let me look," Joanne demanded, snatching the passport from her cousin's hand. After a quick look she announced exasperatedly, "You only have fourteen weeks left. That's all. I told you to check when we first booked!"

"You said I needed thirteen weeks and I have 14 weeks. What's the problem? I have an extra week to convalesce in Spain if anything happens," said Veronica defiantly.

"What do you mean 'if anything happens'? Nothing better happen. Remember last time?"

"Oh, yes, I forgot. How is your leg?" winced Veronica at the memory of the retribution.

"It's fine... now! Except in frosty weather. Tickets?"

"Check."

"Money?"

"Check."

"We're virtually there," said Veronica. "What could possibly go wrong now? It's all out of our hands and in the hands of those amazingly good looking pilots." She nodded towards a group of blue suited, ramrod straight pilots walking the length of the booking hall, surrounded by beautiful members of their cabin teams.

"You can sit back now Jo Jo and relax, knowing you are being looked after by professionals. I hope we're not flying in one of those new Lockheed TriStar planes, but I suppose we can't be fussy as we've only booked economy. Though I'd sooner fly on something that has five stars, or even just four stars."

Joanne's eyes shut and her head went down at the thought of two weeks of endless chatter and annoying opinions.

After talking light heartedly to other holidaymakers as they shuffled back and forth in the zigzag queue, they eventually arrived at the check-in desk. Looking back, the queue seemed just as long as when they'd first arrived.

Joanne slid her case weightlessly onto the conveyor belt alongside the check-in desk. The destination label was threaded through the handle and her designer bag glided smoothly from view.

Veronica, with Joanne's help, managed to lug her bag onto the conveyor belt as soon as Joanne's had disappeared. She had done an excellent job of securing the case by winding tape around and around lengthways and widthways. She had wound tape around so many times it was difficult to tell the colour of the original case, but secure it certainly was.

"Your case is twelve pounds overweight, Madam! That will be an excess baggage fee of £36, please."

"£36? You must be joking!"

"No Madam, it's £3 per pound over the weight allowance."

"Well, I can't pay. That would be all my spending money for the first week!"

"Then you can't fly. Next!" The check-in lady looked over Veronica's shoulder at the next person in the queue and beckoned them forward.

"If I took a few things out would it be OK?" asked Veronica, politely compliant.

"If it was below four pounds overweight then I'd be prepared to turn a blind eye, Madam."

Together, Veronica and Joanne dragged the offending case across to an open area of floor space alongside the queue, where they started to undo the endless rolls of tape. The first article of clothing to come out of the half unwound case was a thick, multi-coloured jumper.

"What the hell do you need this for?" asked Joanne, holding it up for inspection.

"It gets cold in the evenings sitting on the beach with a suitor. I'll wear it on the plane. They aren't going to weigh me, are they?"

"Just as well, you'd probably need two tickets! And this?" Joanne pulled out one of a pair of brand new, pink trainers. "You going jogging?"

"Put those back, I might be invited to go for a walk with someone. Look, I've got to go Joanne, I really need the loo. I need it really badly. I know, I know, before you say anything, I should have gone before."

"You can't go now. You'll just have to hold on."

Ignoring her cousin, Veronica raced around the back of the

queue and sped off to find a loo as fast as her platform soled shoes would allow.

A wicked thought crossed Joanne's mind. Her own case had been within the weight limit and had gone through. She could say to Veronica that she heard the final call for the gate and had to leave Veronica's case at the side of the check-in desk. Veronica could sort the problem of her case out herself, or not. The thought of single occupancy at the hotel was very appealing. But, on reflection, Veronica was family so Joanne resigned herself to the task.

A very cross Joanne pushed the first pink trainer into a nearby bin. Once back to the bulging case with one side curled up, her hand slid inside and pulled out the other pink trainer. That also went into the nearby bin. A yellow high-heeled shoe was next. Rummaging with one arm up to the elbow inside the case, Joanne soon pulled out the other yellow shoe. "Why ever does she pay a fortune for pretty yellow shoes she can only see when she's on the loo?" questioned Joanne. Racing over to the bin again, she stuffed them deep down inside.

Joanne looked up to see if Veronica was anywhere nearby. The check-in lady was watching the performance out of the corner of her eye with a wry smile on her face as she checked in other passengers. She knew exactly what was going on. By this time the queue had joined in too and were all on the lookout. They signalled that the coast was clear.

Another rummage and Joanne found the end of a shawl. A woollen shawl! Who on earth takes a woollen shawl to Spain in the summer time? Out came the voluminous garment after lots of pulling. Into the bin it went. Six chick flick books also went into the bin. Whenever was Veronica going to read six books? If she read one it would be amazing.

Half of the snaked queue were now craning their necks to see what would be pulled out of the case next, and the other half were on the lookout for Veronica.

"Quick, she's coming," shouted one half of the queue in unison, as they saw her hurrying from the other side of the departure lounge.

Joanne stuffed any protruding straps and anticipatory lace garments back into the case and re-attached the tape wherever she could. She then, single-handedly, dragged Veronica's considerably lighter case to the check-in desk and loaded it onto the conveyor.

A cry went up from the queue, "She's nearly here!"

The check-in lady looked at the case, then at Joanne's pleading face, then at the pleading queue.

There was silence. The audience were willing her to be generous. More silence.

The check-in lady was examining the scales and looking at the case. She started to shake her head slowly from side to side. The check-in lady was heightening the theatre of the moment and savouring the tension in her normally tedious job. A groan went up from all the onlookers. Then, quick as a flash she smiled, threaded the destination label through the case handle, and pressed the GO button on the conveyor.

There was a real buzz of appreciation from the queue. Then, quite unexpectedly, she stood up, stepped to one side of her desk and took a bow as the bulging, brown, borrowed suitcase disappeared behind her. There was an instantaneous round of applause and cheers from the delighted onlookers.

Joanne, for her contribution, turned to face the queue and shouted, "Yes!" She punched the air then took a bow, too. The whole queue was clapping her success and were in fits of laughter just as a sweating Veronica in her just in case, thick, multi-coloured jumper rounded the queue.

"What was all that about?"

"No idea," replied Joanne innocently.

"Where's my case?"

"Gone to Malaga."

"Oh, well done, Jo Jo. I knew I could rely on you to talk her into letting it go. It was only a few pounds over anyway."

Joanne stopped in her tracks, turned to Veronica and, at a loss of what to say, shook her head in disbelief, tut-tutted and rolled her eyes skywards. "Stop calling me bloody Jo Jo," she snapped.

Security was, thankfully, a walk in the park, but there was a small, heart stopping incident on their way to the departure gate. They were chatting as they walked, discussing which gin to take with them, when a security guard tapped Joanne on the shoulder. He coughed and said, "Excuse me, Miss." They both turned and Joanne's face went white.

"May I see your passport, please?"

"Well, yes, but what for?"

"May I see your passport please, Miss?" he repeated very courteously.

Joanne was nervous as she opened her matching passport and document bag. She gasped, "It's not there! I must have dropped it. Veronica, did I give it to you?"

"You? Trust me with your passport? Huh, I don't think so."

"You left your passport in one of the security trays, Miss." The very good-looking security guard placed the passport into Joanne's hand and smiled.

Veronica silently grumped, having narrowly missed out on single occupancy for herself for two weeks in Spain. She then felt churlish and uncharitable for even thinking such a dreadful thought.

"It's easily done, Miss. Happens all the time, Miss."

Joanne continued profusely thanking the security guard, seemingly reluctant to let go of his hand. Veronica said a small prayer of thanks that it hadn't been her passport, but smarted at the fact that she had been called Madam at the check-in desk and Joanne had been called Miss time after time by the good-looking security guard.

The leisurely start to the holiday the pair had promised themselves had disappeared with the late taxi arrival and incident at the check-in queue.

Loaded down with two bottles of gin and two bottles of vodka from the duty-free shop, the pair hurried to boarding gate 21 only to hear as they arrived that the gate had been changed to another gate at the other side of the airport.

Joanne's stress level was rising by the moment and Veronica decided to only speak when spoken to.

They helped a confused couple find their way as the woman was becoming really anxious and the man was becoming more and more agitated. If he said to them once that this was their first holiday involving a flight and probably their last, he said it a hundred times.

Veronica reassured them both that they would not miss the plane as everyone in the crowd was hurrying across the airport to the same gate, all weighed down by clinking carrier bags.

Once on the plane there seemed to be about twenty seats not occupied in front of them. Hope blossomed in Joanne's mind that Veronica could spread out on one of the empty rows of seats for the journey and she wouldn't be squashed for the duration of the flight.

It was not to be. Twenty boisterous guys, on the first day of their stag party, noisily filled every vacant seat. Joanne groaned whilst Veronica's eyes lit up.

Veronica could sense party in the air, she could sense a fun time and a possible holiday romance. She had scanned the individuals in the group as they snaked along the plane looking for their seats and decided who would be her first target, her second and, in the worst case, her third. The staggers would only be in the same town as them for a week at the most so she knew she would have to work quickly to score.

Joanne could not have been more opposite in her thinking. Here was noise for the duration of the flight, here was an interruption to her reading schedule, and here was alcohol fuelled juvenile humour. She sent a prayer up to heaven pleading that the group would be staying in another hotel to her and Veronica.

After a predictably raucous flight, Joanne was pleased the landing was incident free and passport control was unexpectedly quick. The transport to the hotel was in a surprisingly smart coach, populated by them, the nervous couple and the twenty staggers, much to Joanne's prolonged chagrin. "Oh, please God, tell me we are not staying at the same hotel as the stag party, please," she whispered again.

But they were. Thirty minutes later their coach lurched to a standstill with a hiss of noisy Spanish air brakes. The twenty loud guys unloaded their motley selection of cases and bags from the coach and jumbled into the hotel foyer, where the disbelieving group were offered non-alcoholic fruit juice. Calls like, "Hey, Manuel, where's the bar?" and "Where can we get some pizzas?" could be heard all over the quiet hotel.

Veronica and Joanne joined the boisterous queue to check in and, after some time, were given their room key. They lugged their cases to the lift and punched in the fourth floor. Right at the end of the corridor, as far as they could be from the lift, was room 408.

"At least none of the rowdy staggers will be passing our room to get to theirs during the early hours of the morning," said Joanne rolling her wheeled case. She was way in front of a puffing and sweating Veronica who was trying to hold her case together as she half carried it and half dragged it, leaving in her wake a trail of adhesive tape stuck to the corridor carpet.

The clean hotel room housed two three quarter beds and a bathroom that smelled of a recent sandalwood and pomegranate disinfectant tsunami. Joanne's inspection included touching the towels to feel their softness. The towels passed. Next came the search for dark, curly, pubic hairs in the shower and basin plug holes. There were none. The appliances received a nod of approval too. The accommodation had passed her painstaking inspection - it was clean and, for the most part, away from the staggers.

Experience had taught Joanne that an effective extractor fan in the bathroom that didn't sound like a noisy two stroke motorbike was absolutely essential when sharing with Veronica. This was on account of her gastronomic experimentation with the local foods and beverages. Joanne clicked the light on and breathed a sigh of relief as the extractor fan whirred silently.

During this thorough inspection, Veronica was unravelling yards and yards of tape from her case beside the single bedroom window, which looked out onto an expansive supermarket car park.

Its security fence was wallpapered by rubbish and waste paper blown by the onshore wind. In the corner of the car park, adjacent to their window, was a sad graveyard of dead supermarket trolleys, some with wheels missing, some with baskets bent beyond recognition, and all with metalwork rusted brown by the sea air.

Joanne sighed thoughtfully to herself as she peered outside. "Well, I suppose it's better for the trashed trolleys to be here in a big heap than in the canals and rivers like home." But there did seem to be an inordinately big heap of them. She assumed that Spanish shoppers must either be poor trolley drivers, excessive over loaders, or perhaps they engaged in supermarket trolley rage. "At least they are out of sight of everyone, except us that is."

A few minutes later there was a squeal of delight as Veronica came out of the bathroom trailing the toilet paper in one hand and a fresh toilet roll in the other. "I've never been in such a posh place," she said as she held up the toilet paper with the last sheet folded neatly into a point. In the other hand she held up the fresh toilet roll with a piece of tissue stuffed carefully into the top to resemble a pink lily. "Wow Jo Jo, this is a real classy hotel."

"You need to get out more, and stop calling me bloody Jo Jo."

5

Christopher and Rosie spent about an hour carefully unpacking, placing all their clothes into the drawers, and arguing over every hanger in the wardrobe. Finally, all their clothes were hung up and their toiletries neatly arranged on the surfaces that surrounded the washbasin, in precise order of usage.

They then decided to explore the hotel before dinner. Taking the lift to the ground floor they ended up looking out at a forest of brushes and vacuum cleaners, and a mountain of laundry, in the basement.

“You must have pressed the wrong button,” snapped Christopher.

“I pressed the correct button as you quite plainly saw,” Rosie retorted slowly and very deliberately. The touch of acid in her voice said to Christopher ‘be careful, don’t push me, I’m very tired too’.

Then, before they could press another button, the lift door closed and it took them back to the fourth floor where Veronica and Joanne joined them in the lift. Veronica explained that Spanish lifts have the ground floor as the first floor, just like America.

Christopher grumped that it made no sense at all, but kept a watchful eye on Rosie. He had experienced her verbal teeth when she was very tired only once or twice before in their years of marriage, and still bore the scars.

The time was about 6.00 pm and sociable Veronica suggested the Gilliams join her and Joanne for a drink in the bar before dinner. A look peppered by shards of glass from Joanne made Veronica back-pedal, suggesting that they may have other plans.

However, Rosie reinforced their gratitude for the help given to them at the airport and on the coach, and said if they didn't feel it was an imposition they would be delighted to join them. Rosie's actual objective was to dilute Christopher's moaning. Christopher, on the other hand, was hoping for a relatively swift meal and an early night - it was their thirtieth wedding anniversary, after all.

Joanne had fourteen days left of her holiday and wanted a slow start, not having to make polite conversation with complete strangers on their very first day. Veronica was just being Veronica.

On hearing it was Christopher and Rosie's wedding anniversary, the barman offered the four of them a complimentary bottle of local sparkling wine.

When that one had been drunk, another followed. Christopher had calmed down, Rosie had mellowed, Joanne was happy to drink on someone else's tab all evening, and Veronica was in, 'it's the first day of my holiday and I'm making every day count' mode.

Forty five minutes later, all the nuts and crisps on the bar had disappeared. Two empty bottles of local sparkling wine, plus four empty glasses, faced the holidaymakers with a decision. The choice was either another round of drinks or to quickly eat something.

The sensible decision was Joanne's. "Let's eat." She also did not want to hear again about what a stressful job it was running a hardware shop, or the escalating price of mouse traps, or the drop in the quality of Chinese manufactured galvanised buckets.

The four of them were led to a corner table in the restaurant by a dream of a waiter, who flirted outrageously with tipsy Rosie behind Christopher's back.

The seasoned cousins understood the process fully: the waiter flirts with the middle-aged wife, and at the end of the holiday receives a fat tip. A thank you hug and kiss for the tip from the waiter ensures the hotel is considered for the holiday makers' following year's trip. The middle-aged wife has a face and a kiss to bring to life her fantasy dreams for a whole year. Everyone wins.

Veronica, the more seasoned predator, walked behind the waiter taking in every aspect of his tight trousers and sharp waistcoat. She nudged Joanne and nodded at the waiter's pert bottom.

Joanne shook her head in disbelief that they had only been in the hotel a short time. Raising her disapproving eyes skyward, she shook her head again and noisily tut tutted.

Their table was positioned with a magnificent sea view. Already lubricated by two bottles of local sparkling wine, the four chatted easily.

The menu was a mix of Spanish and Italian cuisine that the experienced Joanne interpreted for the other three. To cater for the more discerning English palette, chips were served with everything. During the course of the meal the staggers took their places at their prescribed tables, noisily acknowledging Veronica and Joanne.

The wine with dinner was local, rough and free, and slipped down the two seasoned drinkers quickly. It slipped down the two novice drinkers equally quickly, despite them seldom enjoying more than a sherry or two at Christmas time. Lubricated by alcohol, Christopher talked the most in their little group.

"It's our wedding anniversary as you know, so we won't be able to stay with you for long." He winked knowingly at Joanne when he said it. Joanne ignored him. Rosie excused Christopher, raising her eyes and saying, "My husband, he's so predictable, I'm sorry."

The sweet course was followed by the obligatory, complimentary, local spirit that regular holidaymakers to Spain usually declined.

Warnings from Veronica about the local hooch having a tendency to sometimes creep up and attack you in the back of the legs was met with scorn from Christopher. He regaled them about how, many years ago, he used to be in the local darts team who regularly met in the White Lion. (Or was it the Red Cow or the Prince of Stags or something like that? He couldn't remember.)

Veronica and Joanne looked on in amusement as the pair corrected each other's stories, their eyes becoming redder and their voices louder and louder in the restaurant.

The cheese course was a timbale of tastes and smells of

beautifully presented artisan Manchego and Cabrales cheeses. Above the restaurant noise Christopher loudly asked the waiter if they had any cheddar.

He was answered politely by the dream waiter, "This is Spain, Sir, and industrially produced cheeses have not yet reached my beautiful country." Rosie giggled. Christopher was embarrassed.

Coffees were to be served in the lounge area but as Rosie and Christopher rose to walk the thirty yards to the lounge, Veronica and Joanne realised at the same time they had two problems on their hands. Neither Rosie nor Christopher were able to walk without holding onto something solid and, as the restaurant was now full, negotiating a vertical exit was going to be difficult, maybe impossible.

Veronica quickly chose to offer the more slightly built Rosie some help, which was accepted willingly by someone acknowledging that their vision had become hazy, and their legs had little life left in them.

Veronica threaded the compliant Rosie between the tight tables. When they reached the exit she looked back to see how Joanne was faring with Christopher. Not well was her observation. If shards of glass had been fired when Veronica had invited the holidaymakers to join them, then primed and loaded scud missiles were on her way.

It was obvious that Christopher was being more defiant and insisting he did not need Joanne's help ("I was once on the darts team!"), until he tried to stand up and the higher stratosphere made him sit down again abruptly.

By this time the staggers were in full voice at tables all around them but fortunately two of the lads, who had been like bees around honeypots on the plane, offered Joanne their help. Between the four of them, they helped the now completely drunk Gilliams to the lift and all squashed in.

The two staggers were only too happy to help. In the confinement of the lift they introduced themselves to Veronica and Joanne as Daz and Ronnie.

Introductions to Rosie and Christopher were a complete waste of time as both were now incoherent and struggling to focus. Rosie was nearly asleep on Veronica's chest, and Christopher's eyes were tired of trying to focus and all but shut.

On the fourth floor corridor, one of the staggers searched Christopher's pockets for the room key and the unstable group of six stumbled into the room.

Inside, Ronnie leaned Christopher against a wall while Daz put towels all over the bathroom side of Christopher's bed. They set him down with his head on the towels and the waste bin was placed within easy retching distance. The bathroom light was left on. Any furniture obstructing the sprint to the bathroom was removed, for painful, drunken history had taught them both that the shinbone is an accurate device for finding furniture in a darkened room.

It was obvious to Joanne and Veronica that these preparations were a regular occurrence with Daz and Ronnie's friends, as they didn't need to say a word while they rearranged the bedroom. They left Rosie to Veronica and Joanne, who gently laid her on the other bed with a glass of water by her side, some towels over the edge of the bed, and the bin from the bathroom close by.

Satisfied, the four left and gently closed the door. Together they walked to the lift then back to the dining room where Daz and Ronnie invited them to join their group. Joanne was about to decline and settle for a quiet nightcap, but Veronica said they would love to buy them a drink for all their help.

More missiles.

The evening was short lived for Veronica and Joanne as, just as things were beginning to swing, one of the staggers suggested it was time to head on out for the rest of the night. As one the staggers all rose, leaving their tables covered in a forest of empty pint glasses, beer bottles and full ash trays.

Veronica perked up but the invitation was not extended to either of the guests at their table, much to Joanne's delight and Veronica's mortification.

6

The following morning, after a late breakfast, Joanne and Veronica prepared their beach bags for the day. After much searching, Veronica asked, "You seen my trainers, Jo Jo?"

A shrug of the shoulders reinforced Joanne's reply, "Must have fallen out at the Spanish baggage carousel."

Five pesetas each secured two poolside sun beds for the two weeks, and the pair settled down for some serious sun bathing and reading.

After two trips to recover things that had been forgotten, the pair lathered each other in cream to do battle with the sun on their first day in paradise. The umbrella was removed and the two lay in the glare of the full sun, topping up their vitamin D tanks.

"Damn. No sunglasses." Once again, Veronica headed off back to their room.

Veronica was red faced on her return. "Bloody cheek," she growled as she lowered herself onto the protesting sun bed and pulled her bikini bottoms up to tuck in more tummy.

“What can possibly have gone wrong now? You’ve only been gone a few minutes?”

“I haven’t done anything. It’s not always me. I bumped into one of the staggers in the foyer who was up earlier than all the rest. He looked me up and down in my new bikini and said, ‘Good on yer, darling’.”

“And what did you say to him?” asked Joanne curiously.

“I called him a cheeky sod!” snapped Veronica, rearranging her sun bed.

“He probably meant it as a compliment,” suggested Joanne, who had to hide her head in her book as she shook uncontrollably at the comment.

What was left of the morning dawdled towards a long and wet lunch, and lunch drifted into a white wine induced sleep for both of them.

It must have been approaching 3.00 pm when Joanne spotted Rosie peering through dark sunglasses, searching amongst all the sun beds for them. Once spotted, she slowly headed their way. Joanne woke Veronica.

“I just had to come and find you both to apologise for our behaviour last night.”

“It’s fine. We’ve all been there, haven’t we Joanne?” reassured Veronica.

Joanne gave Veronica a sideways look suggesting it was she who had the lion’s share of experience in the matter.

“I don’t know what got into us,” continued Rosie. “Whatever must you think of us? We never drink like that and we have hangovers like I have never experienced before. It’s like bombs going off in my head all of the time. Christopher is still in bed saying he thinks he has food poisoning or more probably a virus! I don't think he will be down for dinner tonight as he had to get up to be sick a few times in the night."

"I expect he was just getting up to let the virus out," said Veronica, not even looking up from her only holiday book.

"Well, I best be getting back to him. He's not a good patient even at the best of times."

"If you decide to come down on your own for dinner tonight then feel free to join us. Don't sit on your own," offered Veronica.

"Thank you. You've both been so kind, but I'll stay and look after him."

Rosie turned and began ambling back to the main hotel. She wasn't out of earshot when Veronica exclaimed loudly to Joanne, 'Typical bloke. Can't take his alcohol and blames a virus. Virus my arse, he was pissed as a rat!"

Joanne and nearby holidaymakers who couldn't help but hear her declaration, all laughed out loud.

Approximately ten hours seemed to be the magic amount of time the staggers needed to recover from the previous night's revelry. Veronica's more earthy theory was that the actual duration was bladder driven and, as the week rumbled on, it was as if an alarm was set in all the staggers' rooms.

Between 3.00 pm and 4.00 pm a range of hangovers tumbled towards the pool. Some already had pints in their hands and others were munching on dustbin lid sized pizzas. From then on boisterous behaviour became the order of the afternoon, and pizzas were often snatched from their unsuspecting owners and used as Frisbees across the pool.

The Frisbee game always degenerated into lads diving off the diving boards to try and catch the pizzas as they were skimmed across the evacuated, empty pool. Jalapenos and slices of salami and ham littered the deep end. Roars of laughter punctuated the stunned poolside silence as staggers bombed off the top board onto mates who were trying to quietly swim.

Wrestling on the edge of the pool was the game of the week, and continued to have the potential of a precursor to a visit to A&E.

By 5.00 pm every day the staggers were the only ones at the pool.

By 6.00 pm happy hour had begun at the poolside bar.

By 7.30 pm they, en masse, headed for the dining room.

All the other holidaymakers understood the staggers' routine and avoided the pool after 5.00 pm, and made sure they were close to finishing their meals by 8.00 pm, for some of the staggers' restaurant etiquette and table manners were in short supply.

The staggers hit the hotel bar until about 11.00 pm and then went out clubbing until 4.00 am, or even later.

They were harmless enough and Joanne and Veronica watched the stamina of individuals wane as the week progressed. Both Daz and Ronnie were seasoned staggers, pacing themselves to last the course. They introduced the stag - a lad named Wilson - to Veronica and Joanne, who both decided a week long stag party in Spain with that lot, who all seemed considerably older than him, was not a good idea.

In the first three days the police had brought Wilson back to the hotel twice. The first time, Wilson had been found handcuffed, in the buff, to the central pillar of the bandstand in the town square, as drunk as a skunk.

On the second occasion, the police had found him drunk, chained and naked in a pedalo, drifting out to sea.

A third incident, that didn't warrant police attendance, was when Wilson fell asleep at the poolside in the late afternoon. The best man tied a firecracker to his foot by a piece of string about a yard long, lit it and waited. When the firecracker went off, the completely disorientated Wilson ran wildly about chased by loud bangs wherever he went.

Unfortunately, he did have to spend a night in hospital as, in trying to escape the incessant bangs, he ran straight into a tree and dislocated his shoulder. The staggers thought it hilarious.

In fact, having met Wilson, Joanne and Veronica decided that marriage for the young lad was probably not a good idea either. Veronica decided his sad eyes reminded her of a squirrel with a nut allergy.

He was only twenty two years of age and already a father of two with another on the way. He looked as if he was still in school and the cheap, blurred tattoos on his skinny arms and legs did nothing to enhance his age or maturity, and would be sorely regretted in later life.

His behaviour screamed immature, adolescent and childish,

and he was continually trying to impress the wrong people. When he was on his own his demeanour was despondent.

What a start in life, thought Joanne.

Daz was the most sensible of the staggers and regularly wanted to return to the hotel long before the rest of them. It often coincided with Joanne being ready to leave the clubs, and they ended up walking back to the hotel together.

Joanne liked Daz. He had a puckish smile and she was intrigued how he acquired his name. She laughed out loud when he explained. His real name was Peter James White but, given the choice by his mates of being called Omo or Daz, he was happy to settle on Daz. She agreed wholeheartedly and chuckled each time the explanation crossed her mind.

Daz chatted with her easily. He explained he was in a loose relationship with a girl and had only been persuaded to join the stag party to make up the numbers by his older brother, who was to be Wilson's best man.

Daz complained bitterly that his brother was a bit of a taker. He described him as, "The sort of guy who is a first out of the taxi and last at the bar type; a seasoned stagger. By the time we return to the UK he'll have spent less than anyone else during the week, but will have drunk more than anyone. He'll have timed his rounds to perfection when the least number of drinks would be needed, or everyone was so drunk they couldn't remember whose round it was anyway."

Joanne was surprised by Daz's derogatory description. She said she thought he looked a very pleasant young man but Daz suggested that just as light travels faster than sound, he gave the impression of being bright until he opened his mouth. "God only knows what he's going to say in his best man's speech."

Daz complained to Joanne that being away from home was the last thing he needed right now as he was at the tail end of his second year of a college course in Business Studies. If he had been at home, he would have been studying all day, every day. He confided in her that he left the clubs early to go back and study in his room, until his noisy fellow staggers returned drunk as skunks anytime between 4.00 am and 6.00 am.

He didn't drink as much as the others, started drinking much later and was ridiculed whenever he started to leave as being a 'lightweight', but all the banter went over his head. Daz did as Daz pleased. Joanne liked Daz. He was mature beyond his years compared with the juvenile behaviour of the other staggers.

The staggers were only due to be there for six days and, as the days raced by, Joanne began to regret Daz would be leaving. She had come to enjoy his company despite him being about four years younger than her. He had depth of conversation, didn't want to show off or drink till dawn, and he was fit!

One evening they walked the long way back to the hotel, along the beach. It was that lovely temperature of the night, and the stillness and silence was a welcome contrast to the head banging music of the club.

They chatted and laughed like old friends and, in the brief conversation lulls, listened to the lapping of the waves that create lasting memories of Spain.

Joanne kicked off her sandals and walked in the sea up to her ankles. Daz kicked off his trainers and followed suit. He asked, "Have you ever swum in the sea at night? There's a strange, mystical magic to it."

Joanne replied, "No chance. I'm too scared to. It doesn't make any sense I know, but when I can't see what's below me in the water, I get nervous and afraid. I think there might be monsters out there in the dark water."

"Would you be afraid if I was out there with you Jo Jo?"

Joanne rather liked the affectionate pet name of Jo Jo when Daz said it. She thought for a long moment, looked into his enquiring eyes and replied, "No."

Meanwhile, seasoned partygoer Veronica could easily hold her own in juvenile company till dawn. She had quickly been given the respect she richly deserved in drinking games and had become an honorary stagger. However, she over-stepped the mark in Joanne's eyes that night as the staggers walked rowdily home.

Joanne had been in bed, alone, since returning from her swim with Daz at 2.00 am. Suddenly, at 5.00 am there was an almighty ruckus outside the hotel. Along with most of the other hotel guests, she went out to see what was causing the noise.

Three supermarket shopping trolleys were being set up to have a four hundred yard race along the promenade, right outside the row of hotels.

Six lads were ready to push the first trolley. The best man was crouched as the passenger, shouting abusive encouragement at his stag party pushers. Six lads were ready to push the second trolley with Wilson draped half inside and half outside the trolley, still with his arm in a collar and cuff and barely conscious. In the third trolley, screaming like a banshee at her pushers, was...Veronica.

The gathered crowd started to count down. Three, two, one...and then they were off!

Each set of pushers crashed their trolley into the other chariots and the shouting was deafening. Pushers zigzagged in front of each other to slow the competition, accompanied by streams of abuse; no wonder the whole road of hotels were outside watching the spectacle, as well as spectators at all the hotel windows! The three trolleys gathered momentum, eventually being abandoned by their pushers for the last, downhill, one hundred and fifty yards.

The trolleys gained speed, their occupants totally out of control and hanging on for their lives. The small wheels were shaking the riders as if they were being driven over cobbles.

The front runners were Veronica and the best man. Wilson was now fully awake and the terror was evident on his face as he narrowly missed lamppost after lamppost. The best man's and Veronica's trolleys had become snagged together and, try as he might, the best man couldn't separate them.

A lone concrete parking bollard loomed in front of them and seemed to lean over and clip the best man's trolley. The two trolleys immediately parted company, both spinning in different directions on the promenade. Around and around they whirled, neither rider knowing which way was forward.

Wilson's trolley missed the offending concrete bollard by the thickness of a cigarette paper and, still gathering speed, continued straight on between the other two whose trolleys had virtually stopped spinning. At the same time they started to reverse down the hill, eventually crashing into the promenade wall at the end of the beach, behind Wilson.

He was then carried back to the hotel triumphant, amid loud cheers and disputes over cheating. High fives ended the day. The spectacle over, all the hotel guests returned to their beds amid a mixture of laughter and tiredness. The promenade road was quiet again.

Joanne considered disowning Veronica that night.

But the reason for the twisted supermarket trolley mountain had now become clear. Those three trolleys would probably end up being taken to the same graveyard in the car park at the back of their hotel, and thrown onto the pile by a disgruntled supermarket manager. How nobody was killed was beyond Joanne.

The next day, all sporting hangovers, the noisy staggers reluctantly boarded a coach and left after lots of kisses and "We must keep in touch!" promises.

There was a peaceful lull until late afternoon when a changeover of guests arrived by coach. Another twenty noisy staggers jumbled out of the coach to Joanne's horror and Veronica's delight. However, once they had all disembarked and were in the lobby, it was announced that they were at the wrong hotel. They all had to climb back on board, pints and pizzas already in their hands.

Joanne breathed a sigh of relief and Veronica pouted until the evening. At the thought of no more trolley races and no more drinking games, Joanne's frostiness towards Veronica was thawing. However, there was a down side for Joanne - no more moonlit swims with Daz. The pair settled in for another week of sun, sand and vodka.

Rosie and Christopher had eventually surfaced in the middle of the first week and, after many apologies, began to enjoy their well-earned anniversary holiday. However, for a day of respite from Christopher's complaints about the hotel and the heat, Rosie handed Christopher a ticket one morning. It was a surprise full day's tour of ancient monuments.

"But there's only one ticket?"

"There was only one left so I thought, as you work so hard for us my darling, you should have it. You deserve a treat."

"Well, thank you. That was very thoughtful. Will you be alright on your own Rosie?"

"Yes, of course I will. My tummy is a bit off today so I don't want to make it worse by being on a coach. You have a lovely time."

Once Christopher had packed for the excursion, they made their way to the front of the hotel and gave each other a peck on the cheek. Excitedly, he boarded the coach for a full day's tour of ancient monuments. A quick wave and the coach was gone.

Joanne and Veronica were having their mid-morning cup of coffee out on the hotel veranda and watched Rosie and Christopher wave goodbye to each other.

"How thoughtful of Rosie," said Joanne.

"The grumpy sod doesn't deserve her," added Veronica, spooning more sugar into her coffee.

The coach hadn't been gone out of the hotel gates five minutes before the dream of a waiter from the first night arrived, complete with a picnic hamper, tight white trousers and crisp white shirt, to lead Rosie to his little open-topped car. Rosie waved back at Joanne and Veronica as the car door was held open for her.

Two cups of coffee stopped mid-way on their journey to open mouths.

"Well, who'd have thought it?" chorused Veronica and Joanne.

7

Back home, peeling and broke, Veronica and Joanne shared a cheap pasta meal one Sunday night at Joanne's. Reminiscing about the various hilarious holiday incidents had petered out, the recriminations about the staggers' chariot race had been forgotten, and their thoughts were drifting towards their respective futures.

Veronica was all holidayed out; she needed a couple of weeks to recover. Partying till dawn every night in the first week, and attempting to drink Spain dry in the second week, whilst living mainly on tacos, paella, bar crisps and peanuts had taken its toll.

Joanne finished reading her last book on the plane home, as scheduled, and had been caught several times by Veronica displaying an uncharacteristic rosy glow. But tonight was different. Tonight was serious.

The future looked bleak for Veronica who was contemplating going back, cap in hand, to her old boss, ready to eat humble pie and ask for her job back. She didn't relish the thought and phrases like, "You bozo" and "You're in fairyland", and the music to Viva Espana, haunted her. Perhaps she should learn to be less petulant in the future.

Joanne, on the other hand, just stared into her drink. Neither woman was in a good place when they considered their futures, but Joanne showed it the most.

"What's the matter, Jo Jo?" Joanne still hated being called Jo Jo and Veronica knew it. "It's not like you to mope about with your head up your bum," said Veronica, as she poured another large gin and tonic for them both and carried them into Joanne's lounge.

"There's nothing wrong," Joanne snapped back.

"You're normally a pretty grumpy cow, but today you look like you've lost a shilling and found a cow pat. You're as grouchy as a bulldog chewing a wasp."

Veronica placed the drink on the side table next to Joanne.

"Oh, don't mind me, it's just the bloody funeral parlour Gordon left me. The bastard."

"But I thought it was a thriving business. I assumed you would be urning loads. Old folk are dropping dead whilst singing carols around their Christmas trees, this winter's flu is forecast to be a humdinger, road accidents are always happening, and autumn fogs come every year - that's why they're called autumn fogs. It looks to me like a full on profession for you."

Veronica waited for a reaction. There wasn't one and she had been around Joanne long enough to know when not to press a gag. She returned to serious mode. "You can't turn around without hearing about someone popping his or her clogs. You must be rolling in it by now."

"Well, I'm not!" Joanne nearly shouted. "The figures just don't add up. We've had the same number of clients as last year but the income has dropped dramatically since Gordon died. It should have gone up because we aren't paying him a wage. There's money coming in and going out all over the place. No order, no accounts, no processes."

"Well, if the numbers don't add up to you, and you being a bean counter by profession, then it will be like me trying to read Chinese."

"Something is seriously wrong, but I can't fathom it out." Joanne shook her head.

"You OK without ice, Jo Jo?" asked Veronica as she poured another drink.

"No, I'm not OK without ice. It's a very good, duty free gin, and the tonic cost nearly as much. It's not lager. Do it properly or not at all. And don't call me bloody Jo Jo."

"OK."

"What I need is someone who can stir up some business for me. Someone who can sell. Someone who isn't afraid of hard work. Someone who would be prepared to work for very little money but move into one of the two flats above the funeral parlour for free. I'm moving into the other one to save some money too."

Veronica's sheep dog ears pricked up at the sound of free accommodation. She was already two months behind with the rent so had nearly used up all her deposit. If she walked out within a month, she would just about be even with the landlord, but that's as far as her planning had reached.

"And what would this hypothetical person have to do to drum up more business? Go around banging on doors shouting, 'Bring out your dead, bring out your dead?' I can sell to the living but I'm not sure how to sell to the dead."

"No, stupid, you wouldn't be selling to the dead."

"Oh, so it is me then, is it? And don't call me stupid!"

"I don't know who it is yet, my mind's in a whirl. I can't think straight. I'll have to sack old Vincent. Do you know that both Vincent and his missus, Elsie, are in their late seventies? I'm sure he's up to something; he's very cagey. Now I'm running the business that'll cut the wages bill, and the casuals will have to take a drop, too. I'm sure I can manage the business as well as Gordon with Elsie the embalmer's help. However, I suppose I'll still need Vincent to drive the ancient hearse and do whatever else he does. I can't do everything. I need someone else out there working for me. Raising the business profile, marketing, selling. Oh, I don't know yet."

"Well, if you think I'm stuffing bandages up orifices, washing dead folk, smearing embalming fluid all over them and then dressing them in their finery ready to be buried, you can think again. I am not, I REPEAT I AM NOT, doing it. Not for you or anyone else. Not for a gold pig will I be an embalmer. Just the thought gives me the creeps."

Veronica shivered visibly and spilled her drink over the beige carpet, rubbing it in with her foot before Joanne noticed.

"You wouldn't have to. Elsie will take care of all that side of things. You, or whoever comes to work for me, would do some undercover selling."

"Undercover selling? Sounds intriguing. How does anyone do undercover selling for a funeral parlour?"

She affected a posh voice, "Hi, my name's Veronica and I

work for a funeral parlour. I know you're not dead yet, but you look pretty poorly to me. Would you mind putting these funeral parlour business cards in all your pockets, including your pyjamas, ready for your family to find when you do go?"

She looked pointedly at Joanne. "Or perhaps I could stand outside the crematorium and suggest to old folk attending friend's funerals that it's hardly worth the bother of them going home!"

"No, that's not what I meant at all and you know it. You used to be some sort of a nurse, didn't you?" Joanne was leading the conversation carefully towards her goal.

"Yes, for a year and a half I was 'some sort of a nurse' but it was a very long time ago, and it didn't end well."

"None of your jobs ever end well! But we could add a bit of colour to your CV, spice it up a bit, and then you could go and work in a private care home."

"A private care home? You must be jesting. Why would I want to go and work in a bloody private care home? The money's hopeless. I hate old people because the men all smell of Old Mice aftershave lotion, and the old ladies smell of out of date perfume that's gone around a dozen raffles. All care homes smell of a cocktail of pee, boiled cabbage, and wet dog. What the hell do I want to go and work in a private care home for?"

"In the first place, how about for some money to pay your way in the form of a wage, so you can buy the takeaways for once, and also the odd bottle of gin? In the second place, to drum up some business for me?"

"And how exactly do I drum up business? The inmates are

hardly the most attentive audience to a sales pitch, are they? Most don't know what day it is and the rest don't care."

"You offer to do regular night shifts at the care home." Joanne realised this plan was a more difficult sell to Veronica than she first envisaged.

"Nights? Regular nights? Now you really must be joking," said Veronica setting her glass down, getting up from the settee and walking over to the window. "This idea gets worse! Have you ever done regular night shifts, Jo Jo? I don't suppose they have many accountants working on regular night shifts, do they? And if they did, they wouldn't be doing them long. I know I'm not much of a mourning person - get it? Get it? Not a mourning person? Oh, never mind, but I hate nights worse than early mornings. I can't sleep at all during the day, my stomach blows up like a balloon, I have wind like you wouldn't imagine, and I'm as grumpy as a bear."

Joanne let the pun fade away and continued her persuasive rhetoric. "You had no problems sleeping during the day on holiday as I recall. Nobody will notice if your stomach blows up, trust me. You have wind any time wherever you are, and you can be a tad tetchy anytime, as your ex-boss, your previous ex-boss and your previous, previous ex-bosses could all testify."

"Has anyone told you that you can be a bit insensitive Jo Jo? Couldn't I do a mix of shifts?"

"No!"

"Couldn't I do a couple of months and just see how it goes?"

"No! When you're fully established as the night shift nurse or manager then you can set about sorting things out."

"Sorting what things out? You're not selling this brainwave idea of yours to me very well are you? Remind me again, what is it that I have to sort out?"

"You know," Joanne said, raising her eyebrows.

"No, I don't know. I'm doing the worst shift in creation for a pittance. I'm working in a care home with old folk, many of whom will need everything doing for them, and then in my spare time I have to sort things out? Sort what things out?" Veronica stood facing Joanne with her hands on her hips, waiting for an explanation.

"You can be really thick sometimes, Veronica. Just don't give the patients the right bloody tablets, or give them too many, or none at all. Whatever you feel is necessary to do the job. You don't have to do it for long, and if you're clever nobody will ever know. Once their soul has gone to the big care home in the sky, you make sure the family come to me for the funeral arrangements."

"What? I can't believe you just said that!" Veronica turned again to look out of the window, gathering her thoughts.

She turned back to face Joanne when the enormity of the suggestion hit her. "You must be off your rocker. I call murdering old folk in their beds considerably more involved than just 'sorting things out'. My next holiday will be in the bloody nick with that light fingered accountant you spent months trying to snuggle up to. Look where breaking the law got him."

"No, you don't understand. Any trouble and you move on to another local care home where you hurry all the vulnerable ones there along a bit."

"And what risks will you be taking whilst I'm out stuffing old folk with tablets they don't need morning, noon and night? I expect you'll be wrestling big heavy ledgers and coffee and fancy brochures and the like from nine 'til five. Real risky stuff!"

"I'll tell you what I'll be doing," said Joanne, calmly. "First, I'll be sorting out all the funeral parlour business administration and finances, and then I'll be tackling the very time consuming task of looking after the clients in a sympathetic and empathetic way."

Veronica involuntarily coughed out loud at the words sympathetic and empathetic.

Undeterred, Joanne continued. "Then I'll be ensuring all their wishes are reflected in the funeral proceedings, such as musical requests and special tributes. When all that's done, I'll be arranging the funeral vehicles, order of service, floral tributes, and choice of coffin or caskets. Have you got the foggiest idea how many different types of casket there are?"

"Yeah, yeah," responded an incredulous Veronica. "I'm sure you'll be rushed off your feet."

"I haven't finished yet. After the funeral service, I'll be arranging for the ashes to be scattered. You have no idea where some people want their cremains to be scattered. Off bloody mountaintops, at sea, in old factories, off river bridges, over family graves, in a columbarium, on football pitches...I nearly refused one outrageous request the other day. A woman wanted her husband's ashes thrown into a sewer because she hated him that much! After much persuading I relented and said we would reluctantly do it, but we didn't. I just flushed the ashes down the loo by the foyer. I said she could be assured he had disappeared down a main town sewer for I had personally dispatched him. We charged her a hefty premium for the service. She was very happy."

Joanne continued on, "Then there are the obituary cards and thank you cards that need sending out to the correct addresses, and I'll be equally as busy accepting the donations for the nominated charities in lieu of flowers." Joanne finally took a breath. "Oh, and I nearly forgot, we need to check for a new-fangled medical contraption called a pacemaker now."

"Why?"

"Because they have a tendency to explode in the crematoria at very high temperatures."

Before Veronica had a chance to respond, Joanne started on a different tack. "Anyway, you'd be hopeless at it. Let's face it, empathy isn't your strongest forte is it? You don't have a sympathetic bone in you. Look at that poor gentleman the other day who had just seen his cat run over by a car and squashed all over the road. What did you say as he sat on a nearby wall with tears running down his cheeks? 'You'll just have to man up and get another cat. There's plenty in the RSPCA, you'll never know the difference.'"

Veronica opened her mouth to protest but Joanne continued.

"And there was that honeymoon bride who lost her wedding ring in the sea in Spain only two days into married life. She was absolutely distraught. Inconsolable. Everyone else was holding their breath and diving down in the sea and hunting for the ring in the sand. What did you say to her with your pina colada in one hand and a fag in the other? 'Never mind, dearie, you haven't had the ring long have you? It's not as if you'd grown attached to it, is it?'"

"They're different situations Joanne and you know it. I didn't instigate any of those misfortunes."

"You wouldn't be causing the old folk in the home any misfortune either, more...speeding up their departure."

"I'm not sure Jo Jo. I'll have to think about it."

"Well, don't take too long. Someone else will jump at the chance. There are a million people unemployed at the moment and a couple of them are already on my short list."

"Free accommodation and all bills paid?" Veronica asked again after a minute.

This was the first sign Joanne was getting anywhere in the discussion. A couple more incentives and she knew the deal would be done. "Yes, and I'll throw in the use of the company car at weekends. And...and...I'll give you 10% of the profit of the business."

"Joanne, you've got to be consistent. A couple of minutes ago you said the funeral parlour isn't profitable," countered Veronica.

"It isn't profitable now but with us working together, me on the inside and you on the outside, we can't fail. We'll make loads of money and, in any case, you don't have a job to go back to after telling your boss he was a bozo and he could shove his job."

"That's a bit harsh."

"But it's true, isn't it? Well, it's decision time."

"I'm not sure. It's a big decision."

"Remember, over a million unemployed..."

"I know, I know, but that will soon go down because it's the first time a woman's led a major political party, thank God."

Joanne could see Veronica was teetering on the edge of agreeing to her proposal. She just needed one more nudge. "How about 20% of the profit, the accommodation and bills paid for, and the use of the company car during the evenings and at weekends? And I don't mean the hearse. If you really don't want to do the care home stuff then you do the embalming and dressing the corpses and I'll go into the care homes."

"No, no, NOT a bloody chance. I'll do the care home bit and you do whatever it is you have to do with the bodies."

"OK then, it's a deal." Joanne silently breathed a sigh of relief. "Now, we both need another drink. I want ice in it and I do want a lot more gin in the glass."

As Veronica walked out into Joanne's tiny kitchen to prepare the drinks she shouted back, "Well, I never thought I would ever be working in the burial game. I was looking for something more exciting, something with a bit of fun in it. There's no fun in funerals."

There was a pause then, at exactly the same instant, both women shrieked with uncontrollable laughter.

8

Veronica drew up in the taxi outside the Bethesda Care Home, a beautiful old house set in its own grounds overlooking the sea on the south coast. The building was probably two hundred years old, and its grandeur was not lost on Veronica.

The name Bethesda - House of Mercy - was an apt name for a care home, Veronica decided.

The front of the magnificent house was covered in bay windows from floor to ceiling, no doubt allowing masses of light into the front rooms. Wisteria wove its way across every window lintel of the ground floor, its deep blue flowers tumbling down, exuding its heavy summer fragrance.

The paint outside was fresh and white, and the gravel drive had been recently raked. The flowerbeds were tended as well as a hotel's gardens. This was no down and out cheap care home, this was a top of the range example.

Secretly admiring Joanne's choice, Veronica pushed the worn ceramic button in the front porch and prepared to meet the care home's manager.

"Veronica Sidero Puxworthy, you say? Flat seven, Canterbury Road?" confirmed the manager, as she led Veronica into her oak panelled office.

"Yes, that's right, but I'll be moving in a few weeks so when I'm settled I'll let you know the new address."

"Thank you. Is it Veronica or Sidero you like to be called?"

"Veronica will do nicely, thank you." Sometimes Veronica hated her mum's stupid sense of humour. Fancy calling your plump daughter a nymph, and an evil nymph at that, just because you heard the name on a TV soap opera once and liked it!

"May I ask, have you worked in a private care home previously, Veronica?"

"Oh yes, several. Mainly in the London area, but I wanted to get out of the rat race and daylight robbery of housing rents. I love the area here and I've always wanted to work near the sea, to be able to smell the ozone, and the seaweed, and hear the seagulls again. We used to come here every year for holidays when I was a little girl, and I've very fond memories of playing on the sand, splashing in the sea, and collecting shells. I love the sea, don't you?"

The care home manager smiled, which Veronica took as a signal to continue.

"On the very last evening of our holidays my mum, dad, gran and sister used to go to the ice cream parlour on the promenade for a treat. It's called Caruso's. I was amazed when I saw that it's still there. Even now the ice cream looks amazingly tempting, despite the dust on some of the ceramic displays, and inside it doesn't look to have changed one bit. Well, it rounded off each holiday for us all before returning up north."

Veronica prattled on, lost in her memories.

"When we were old enough, my sister and I were allowed to order a knickerbocker glory. You know, the one in a glass shaped like a vase with cream on the top in a great big swirl, different coloured ice creams all the way down mixed with tinned fruit, and a cherry right at the bottom. At that age we had to stand on chairs to be able to use the long handled spoons."

The conversation roamed around the benefits of living by the sea for a full twenty minutes. Veronica was happy to chat on the subject as long as possible, for her CV was a work of fiction in the main. The original had been considerably doctored by Joanne, who had a flair for poetic licence and fantasy.

Veronica did struggle a little with Joanne's entry under the heading of hobbies on her CV, especially about travel. Joanne had written: *I enjoy immersing myself in the culture, food, wine and raw sensations of Mediterranean countries.*

Veronica hoped the care home manager wouldn't want her to expand on any of her 'raw sensations' of Spain, as some were still very fresh in her mind. Any reference to raw holiday sensations and Veronica was likely to disappear into a mist of delightful memories, and would find it difficult to concentrate on the matter in hand for some time.

For an activity, Joanne had inserted archery on Veronica's CV. Joanne said she needed to be a bit quirky to make her stand out from all the other candidates.

She dismissed any of Veronica's dissension, being adamant

that it didn't matter one jot what you put down on the form, for interviewers never get down to asking questions about hobbies or activities in a job interview. So, based on that comment, Veronica had only done the scantest of research.

However, the exception always proves the rule and, sure enough, there was a question about Veronica's archery prowess. It threw her momentarily.

Prior to the interview all she knew about archery was that Indians and Robin Hood used bows and arrows. She blagged her way through the answer by expounding the merits of the English yew or boxwood longbow against the latest fibreglass competition bows adorned with pulleys and tensioning devices. She even surprised herself how much she could remember from just one read of the Encyclopaedia Britannica.

What Veronica didn't realise was that the care home manager couldn't believe her good fortune that such an experienced care home assistant had dropped into her lap, especially one who appeared happy to do the night shift and, even better, one who didn't come through an agency with its inflated costs. Veronica Sidero Puxworthy would solve many of her problems in one go.

The final question was asked hesitantly by the care home manager. "I'm sorry to have to ask you this very personal question, Veronica, but after an embarrassing recent appointment of another care home assistant, which did not end at all well, I have been instructed by the owners to ask the same question of every candidate." She paused, then enquired, "How often do you go to the pub for a drink?"

"Oh, that's an easy one," confidently answered Veronica with her fingers crossed behind her back. "Infrequently."

"For my notes, is that one word or two?"

"Just the one," smiled Veronica.

"I think I can say here and now that, barring problems with your references, you can have the job," the manager returned her smile, visibly relieved. "Now, I'll give you a tour around the home."

"Thank you very much," replied Veronica, shaking the manager's hand.

Part one completed, thought Veronica. That will keep Joanne off my back for a while.

The tour around the home with the manager started outside with all the beauty of the old house and its history, as though the care home manager needed to sell the location to Veronica.

Inside, the tour continued along the lines of all the best staff amenities like a well equipped kitchen, period furnished rest room, and a small gym. The gym was completely lost on Veronica.

They continued along the sweeping, high-ceilinged corridors, laid with thick, footstep-silencing carpets, lit by crystal chandeliers, to see some of the residents.

Veronica noted the care home manager referred to the residents more as in-mates rather than patients. The culture of the care home was beginning to form in her mind and it was not one she particularly liked. The manager's coded introductions allowed Veronica to quickly identify those not expected to be at the care home long.

But it was early days. Veronica, despite her hard exterior, was disappointed when the manager spoke about residents within their hearing distance as though it didn't matter if they heard. It was par for the sector though, she reminded herself.

More importantly, and back to the task in hand, the care home manager gave Veronica an insight into the reasons for some of the tablets patients were taking late at night and early in the morning. She explained the drugs round would form part of Veronica's duties once her probation period was over.

Some tablets were for calming residents, others were for diabetic control or to combat water retention, and some tablets were to ensure the night staff had a quiet night. Some were for no purpose at all, but were charged at a hugely inflated price. "I expect you know how it works from the other care homes," was a regular comment from the manager.

Veronica quickly identified one old gentleman called George as her first mark. George was a very pale-complexioned man in his late seventies, fast asleep in bed in the middle of the afternoon. His expansive room was covered with photographs of his grandchildren. The manager described George as, "A bit of a problem when he first arrived with some of the younger nurses, but you won't have any trouble will you?"

Veronica took exception to the comment, but let it go.

"We keep him on ten milligrams of Mogadon every evening and morning. Better he sleeps his last days through rather than embarrass himself and cause us a lot of bother. His family are loaded so we want to keep him here as long as possible and on expensive medication. You understand, don't you?"

Veronica, still smarting from the 'younger nurses' comment, smiled weakly and nodded that she understood the score.

Three days later, Veronica was sporting an employment contract and a very fetching Lincoln green, care assistant's uniform.

She began work alongside an elderly, regular, night shift manager who Veronica assumed had been at the Bethesda Care Home ever since the original house was first built. Her name was Rosalind and she had made it eminently clear at their first meeting she only responded to Nurse Rosalind.

On her first night shift with Nurse Rosalind, they walked the dimly lit corridors together. Veronica was allowed to walk one step behind her superior and believed she now knew how World War One student nurses must have felt when accompanying Florence Nightingale on their shifts.

Nurse Rosalind knocked gently on each bedroom door in turn, opened them, and peeped in. If there was no noise they switched off the lights, or went inside and turned off the TVs. Out of the thirty residents, only two were still awake. Nurse Rosalind had already done the drugs round. Veronica wondered if there was a link.

The next night, Nurse Rosalind explained she had favourite patients, and then there were others. George was in the others group and it showed. Veronica was shown how to select the drugs for him and how to administer them.

Overseen by Nurse Rosalind, Veronica chatted to him as she chatted to every other patient, whilst giving a very sleepy George his night medication. She was watching out for any wandering hands but there were none. In fact, she found him to be a lovely old gentleman. "Don't get too close,"

Veronica quietly warned herself. “Remember why you’re here.”

At midnight, Nurse Rosalind and Veronica sat together in the rest room for a meal. Between mouthfuls, Nurse Rosalind started to quiz Veronica on where she had worked, where she’d enjoyed working the most, and where she’d hated the most and why.

Veronica could be a bit of a fabricator, but on this occasion she stuck as close to the truth as she could. Detailing her nursing experience, she only changed the fact that she had worked as a nurse in a hospital instead of a care home. She reminded herself that fabricators needed to have good memories.

Her father’s words always came flooding back as he coldly recited Walter Scott’s poem, ‘What a tangled web we weave, when first we practice to deceive’. The memory of it still sent a shudder down her back.

As well as visiting other patients, Veronica was directed to go to George’s room again in the morning to administer his first drugs of the day. When she woke him his demeanour was sluggish, nearly drunk. She imagined it to be a result of the tablets, and shortly after she had seen him to the toilet and back to bed he was fast asleep again.

The same procedure happened night after night, and Veronica’s attention focussed more and more on George’s life, such as it was.

Suddenly, on the day her probation period finished, Nurse Rosalind went off sick. Veronica believed she wouldn’t have gone off sick if she, the cavalry, hadn’t arrived on the scene to take some of the strain.

As Veronica's CV said she was qualified to administer drugs, she was to become the night nurse in charge, with a trainee helper to comply with safety regulations.

"Any problems, don't hesitate to ring me," assured the care home manager.

The first night she was in charge, Veronica found she just couldn't give the wrong dose of tablets to the vulnerable, old, gentleman called George. She just couldn't do it. He was kind and gentle and only suffering from a massive overdose of sleeping tablets.

Despite everything she and Joanne had talked about, she just couldn't do it. Joanne had agreed that George seemed a very suitable candidate and as he probably only had a few days left, he'd never know what they were planning. Veronica had since secretly decided she wouldn't hasten his departure from this world. Instead, she would let nature take its course.

That night Veronica gave George two yellow sweets instead of his regular tablets. They looked identical to the ones he was supposed to have.

However, when Veronica went in to see him the next morning he was yawning and half sitting up in bed, saying that this was the first morning for as long as he could remember that he hadn't woken with a blinding headache.

Two more yellow sweets were administered before Veronica went home.

That evening, Veronica asked at the shift handover if George was still with them. "Certainly," was the answer, quickly followed by, "but please don't get your hopes up. Often a sudden, unexplained improvement in a resident's health is an indicator of an early demise."

Nature's decision...won't be long now, went through Veronica's vindicated head.

Later, George didn't need any help taking his milky drink and tablets, and wished her good night when she left the room.

In the morning he didn't need as much help to get to the bathroom as he previously had, and she noticed that he pushed the door to, giving himself a little privacy. A sure sign he was more in charge.

When Veronica went to check on him the following morning he was out of bed and shaving himself. This wasn't the plan. This wasn't the plan at all. Joanne will go crackers, thought Veronica.

She and George had a chat and he asked if she would arrange for the local barber to call to give him a haircut. Veronica was astounded.

In less than a week this frail old man, who was patently near death, had become an upright gentleman. Not ready for the coffin at all. His parchment skin and pallid complexion now had traces of life in it, and there was some colour creeping into his cheeks. He now sat in an armchair looking out over the garden, and asked her if she would accompany him on a little walk to see the roses more closely.

The next evening, when she had completed her rounds, she spent a little more time with him. He was lucid and talked at length about his old job in the Army.

He certainly looked like a different person with his new haircut, clean-shaven appearance, and perfectly trimmed moustache. No longer did he sport a busy nurse's clumsy attempt at shaving a man, leaving random tufts of beard on his chin and giving the impression of a rat looking through a toilet brush!

George shared with Veronica that he'd asked his daughter to bring some of his good clothes to wear. He was heartily sick of wearing jogging bottoms. Never in his life had he ever looked so scruffy.

He wanted to be back in his own cavalry twill trousers, with creases on which one could sharpen a pencil. He didn't want to wear a grey, sloppy T-shirt for one more day, but wanted to wear a crisp, white shirt that had been pressed with care, and a jacket and a tie.

The next night Veronica didn't recognise him. Smart wasn't the word. He walked taller along the corridor, he spoke fluently, and he was proud of his appearance. He asked Veronica to come and sit with him in his room when her chores for the night were complete.

"I'll come straight to the point. There's no need to give me any more yellow sweets instead of my regular medicines."

Veronica gulped.

"I haven't taken the last few days' worth and, before you say anything, I promise not to tell anyone. They've all had the royal order of the flush."

"Thank you," said Veronica. "I'd be in hot water if you did and would probably lose my job. What's more, I have a handbag full of packets of sweets I don't like, all with the yellow ones taken out."

They both laughed out loud.

"I'm leaving this care home tomorrow, thank God, and the old witch of the night," George told Veronica. "I was poorly when I came in seven weeks ago and she has been dosing me up with sleeping tablets ever since. I don't think my body could take many more. One morning soon, you just wouldn't have been able to wake me. Then the care home manager would have said to my daughter, 'There, see, I told you so. He died peacefully in his sleep, the best way to go at his age.' No, it's not the best way to go; virtually unconscious through drugs all day long, just because she can't be bothered to make an effort and treat each person as an individual."

"Forgive me for asking but weren't you a bit of a naughty boy with some of the younger nurses when you first came in here?" Veronica ventured.

"I wish! For goodness sake, I'm seventy two years old, not twenty two. I used to be a bit of a lad with the ladies once, but that was a long time ago. I'll tell you exactly what happened," said George.

"One evening, when I first came in here, Nurse Rosalind - the old witch of the night - was trying to push tablets down me and I refused to take them. She's obviously not used to anyone contradicting her. When she failed to get me to take them she didn't want to lose face as an experienced nurse in front of the other staff, so she fabricated the sexual harassment report. In her dreams! Not even under sedation would I have ever gone anywhere near her. And young? Where's the young bit? She's older than me! So, failing to get me to take the tablets normally, she must have put the crushed tablets into some soup or my milky evening drink. Once under the influence of the first set of sleeping tablets, it was easy for her to just keep me topped up. That's until you came along. It's funny, but do you know that pyjamas make you deaf?"

"What? Pyjamas make you deaf? What do you mean?" asked Veronica.

"Yes, pyjamas make you deaf. When I first came in here I was in a bad way, but whilst wearing a jacket, shirt, tie and trousers everyone spoke to me normally. The moment I put pyjamas on everyone expected me to be deaf and started shouting at me. Except you. Now I'm in civvies everyone is talking normally again."

Veronica laughed. "Where will you go?"

"My daughter has three children and just couldn't manage when I was so ill, as she works full time. Now I'm her old dad again and fighting fit she's happy to have me back, living in my old room. I've so missed the children."

"Good for you."

"I think I would probably be dead by now if it hadn't been for you. The old witch of the night would have seen to it. I owe you a huge debt of gratitude, so I want you to accept this cheque. It's not much, but it's what I would have spent in here for the next five or six weeks until I died. I'd prefer you to have it rather than the care home. I've discussed it with my daughter and she totally agrees. My daughter wants to take the care home on for attempted murder, but I don't want to press charges. I just want to go home."

"I…I can't accept any money from you; it wouldn't be professional." Veronica was choking over the words but could hear Joanne in her ear shouting 'Snatch his hand off!' "I'd lose my job if anyone found out about it."

"You must. I insist," said George, pushing the cheque back into Veronica's hand.

As she was stumbling over more words, she opened the folded cheque and her bottom jaw dropped open. The cheque was for £5,000. "I can't, it wouldn't be right, it's far too much."

"I insist," George reiterated.

"Well, if you are really sure, and only if you are absolutely sure, then thank you very much, and thank your daughter too. I never expected anything. I was just doing my job."

"You're welcome. Now, I can tolerate just one more night in this prison and then tomorrow I'll be back in my own bed. It's a huge thank you from my daughter, my grandchildren, and from me."

George was gone when Veronica arrived at work the next day and she already missed him. His room was bare; all of his photos had been removed and the bed had been stripped down to the mattress, ready for its next victim.

She and Joanne had an almighty row over the outcome of George, with Joanne shouting at her that she was there to help him snuff it, not to help him recover and run around like a dog with two willies!

After the outburst Veronica was so very pleased; she had told Joanne that the cheque was for only £3,000, hence £1,500 each.

9

The following night Veronica was quietly doing her rounds as her assistant was in the staff room having a smoke.

She crept into the bedroom of an elderly lady who she didn't believe would be with them much longer. Her name was Eunice. A quiet chat about Eunice's plans couldn't do any harm, could it? Veronica thought to herself, and Eunice might even be the first patient who went on to Joanne's parlour. Veronica could do with a win to keep Joanne off her back.

Chatting was what Veronica did well. She was always welcome with the patients as light relief from the tedium of the day's routine and solitude. There was also the unspoken, cold realisation by patients that this was the best life they could expect until they were called.

As Veronica went about her nursing duties in the bedroom, she and Eunice chit-chatted about the care home, its lovely grounds, how long Eunice had been there, and how she quite liked the lovely old house.

However, the food was Eunice's most contentious complaint.

She expressed the view that the food wasn't amazing because there was so little variety. In fact, on reflection, she thought it was poor. Veronica had long since learned to let patients have their rant, for if she argued the issue it would be raised every time she entered the bedroom.

Eunice's rant continued, "An identical breakfast everyday of cornflakes and toast leaves much to be desired of the chef's creative talents. Are there no eggs? Is there no bacon? Are there no kidneys? A mid-morning break of coffee and a single ginger nut biscuit at 10.30 am seems to be the limit of his culinary capability. Why aren't there any custard creams or chocolate fingers? Would a Viennese whirl be out of the question?"

Veronica was beginning to side with Eunice about the food.

"There are seven different lunches. The same every Monday, the same every Tuesday, the same every Wednesday, and so on, every single week. Oh, what I wouldn't do for a sandwich. A cheese sandwich on white bread with real butter."

Eunice concluded the food was a real disappointment for the price she was paying at the care home, and her final complaint was that it was mostly bought in pre-prepared. "Mind you," she chuckled, "it doesn't matter too much to me that it's pre-prepared, for at my age I'm happy to eat food that is packed full of as many preservatives as possible!"

Veronica laughed out loud.

The old lady said she had been in the Land Army. She had then moved away from the south coast after the war to become a teacher, then a lorry driver, a doctor's receptionist, the bursar of a private school and, finally, a farmer's wife.

Her life's history was fascinating as she recounted exploit after exploit.

Veronica listened in awe; she believed her own life to have been a bit colourful, but compared with this delightful lady it had been black and white. Eunice had ended up in the Bethesda Care Home because, according to her GP, her organs were beginning to give out on her. Apart from one recently discovered nephew called Denis, she had no other family to care for her.

The following night, Eunice was waiting to share a secret with Veronica. She confessed quietly, from behind a cupped hand, that she hoped nobody minded but when all was quiet in the home, she had a little tipple every night. She showed Veronica a half empty whisky bottle.

"My nephew, Denis, brings me a bottle in every week. I didn't even know I had a nephew until he turned up. Apparently, he was an offspring of my brother who worked abroad most of his life. But even my brother is long gone now. I'm the only one left, except Denis that is. He's such a good boy. Each night when all is quiet, I go under the covers and have a good old swig of Denis's whisky. I hope you aren't going to tell on me, are you? I do feel naughty."

"I won't tell on you, if you let me have a swig as well," Veronica promised.

The excited Eunice suggested, "You get a glass then and we'll have a party. It's such a thrill not to be drinking alone."

"Are you having fun?" Veronica asked.

"Absolutely! It's just like having a party when I was a child," Eunice squeaked. She scurried around her bedroom in her flowing nightie, and Veronica smiled at how much pleasure the so-called party was giving her.

Two glasses were washed and dried, and the old lady poured Veronica two fingers. The smoky whisky went down a treat, despite it having a slightly sweet taste for Veronica's liking.

Mind you, Veronica was hardly a connoisseur of whisky. She regularly downed half a bottle of vodka or gin as 'prinks', as she called them, but whisky seemed to be in a different league. She watched as the old lady downed hers and immediately jumped into bed.

"If I don't get straight into bed, I fall over," she laughed, and was quickly asleep.

Veronica finished the last couple of drops in her glass, gently tucked in and wished the already sleeping Eunice goodnight, and went back to her office to read Eunice's health notes.

Mrs Eunice Broadbent-Smith, aged 75.
Mrs Eunice Broadbent-Smith is suffering from advanced cardiomyopathy.
On no account should she be given caffeine drinks, undiluted fruit juices, or strong chocolate drinks.
Alcohol will aggravate the condition considerably and should be avoided at all costs.

Veronica started to read the document again as it wasn't sinking in. The words were not as clear as the last time she read them. In fact, she was having some trouble focussing on the words at all.

The next thing she knew, the trainee helper was roughly waking Veronica at 6.00 am.

"What the hell? Why didn't you wake me?" Veronica shouted.

"I was asleep as well."

"Right, race around and see that everyone is OK. Check if the bell has been rung and I'll do the drugs round. Then get breakfast ready really quickly. Got it? And not a word to anyone."

The helper rolled her eyes. "I'm not stupid."

Veronica raced off to Eunice's room and was relieved to find her just waking up, holding her head and complaining of a headache.

Veronica popped into the bathroom and recovered one of the glasses from the previous night, which still had a few drops of the whisky in. She secreted it in her uniform and returned to do the drugs round.

When she woke up again later in her funeral parlour flat with her head still pounding, she reflected on the previous night's experience. She decided to investigate the contents of the glass. One of Joanne and Veronica's friends was a hospital doctor and, after a bit of persuading, Joanne offered to ask him to have a look at the liquid.

The next day the hospital doctor rang asking where Joanne had acquired the liquid. She fobbed him off about it being in a coffin of a man from the South Pacific, and commented that it was strange why anyone would want it cremated with their loved one. "Perhaps it was to speed him on to the afterlife?" she said.

The doctor reported that the base of the liquid was a concoction originally brewed in Samoa as a hallucinatory drug. It was a powerful heart stimulant and rated amongst some of the strongest natural drugs in the world.

Veronica could verify that, for her head was still banging like a drum two days after drinking the liquid. The doctor's comment that, "A teaspoonful would knock out a bullock for a couple of days," did nothing for Veronica's self-esteem. He added, "If you are ever offered this at a party, steer very clear. You won't know where the next few days go!"

When Veronica and Joanne were alone, they discussed what to do. Joanne was all for doing nothing, letting the drug do its worst to Eunice and then, because she had no family except Denis, they would automatically have her funeral business.

Veronica pointed out that Joanne had inadvertently alerted the hospital that this drug was local and if Eunice's body had a post mortem, which seemed to be standard practice at the care home, the drug would be swilling about inside her like a lake. There was a slim chance that Eunice's post mortem could be performed by a pathologist who would send a sample to be analysed. They wouldn't miss the connection to Joanne's sample, and the newspapers would scream of a new drug scare in town, centred round the care home and her funeral parlour.

The police would be all over them like a rash.

Joanne considered the quandary for the same length of time it took to down a gin and tonic and then said, "I'll take the risk."

Veronica nodded. "OK, on your head be it."

Despite her conversation with Joanne, on her way to work the next evening Veronica called in at the off-licence and bought a bottle of single malt whisky.

Once at the care home, she poured half the whisky into a clean bottle for Eunice and topped it up with water. The other half she popped into her bag to take home.

When Veronica knocked at the bedroom door Eunice was ready with two glasses, and two fingers of Denis's hooch were in each glass. Veronica suggested they tried another whisky, washed the hooch glasses thoroughly, and refreshed the glasses with her watered down, single malt whisky. Eunice downed hers and quickly jumped into bed.

"Which do you prefer?" asked Veronica.

"Well, yours is so much smoother, smells better, tastes better and doesn't look as cloudy as Denis's, but my nephew would be so upset if I told him not to bring any more."

"How about this then? You accept his whisky gratefully but tell him you never take any until bedtime, and I'll replace it every week with a decent bottle? He'll never know. Deal?"

"Deal."

The next day Veronica called at the care home during the afternoon on the pretext of having left her purse. It was Denis's regular visiting day and time. He was just leaving.

"How is she today then, Denis?"

"As well as can be expected," replied a surprised Denis at the mention of his name.

"My name is Nurse Veronica and I'm the regular night nurse here."

"Oh, Eunice says she likes you."

"And how was Samoa then, Denis?"

The nephew stopped in his tracks, looking at Veronica quizzically.

"I hear they engage in some interesting ceremonies."

"What are you talking about?" he snapped. "I don't know anything about Samoa."

"Well, from what I've read the Samoans administer a drink that induces a hallucinogenic condition. It has all sorts of other effects on the young, but they can take it. They never use it on the old or the infirm because it induces a heart attack." She said the last few words really slowly.

"I don't know what you mean. I don't know what you're talking about. Samoa? I don't even know where Samoa is."

"Oh, I think you do, Denis, and if you bring another bottle of the stuff in here, I'll pass the last bottle on to the police with your fingerprints all over it. I suggest your intentions are dishonourable, so go and find some other helpless old lady to play your dirty tricks on you lying, despicable toad."

"I'll sue you for defamation of character, and slander, and libel, and anything else I can," snarled Denis as he tried to push past the immovable Veronica.

"Go ahead. Do your worst. Want me to get you a brief? Oh, I forgot, my ex is in the drugs squad. Before I mention it to him, me and the other nurses here will beat seven bells out of you if you ever step foot in this place again, or any other care home in the area. Got it?

Dennis didn't know what to do. He didn't believe that

anyone could have found him out, but he wasn't prepared to take a chance with this formidable nurse. He menaced at her and turned to leave.

Veronica had been menaced by the best of them, so Dennis was an amateur to her. "Goodbye Denis. Oh, and have a nice day."

After Denis had been taken care of, Veronica was in a quandary. The thought of despatching old folk before their time did not sit well with her. Was there some other way she could satisfy Joanne's plan without hurting anyone?

She decided to spend her time, rather than hastening departures, by persuading residents' relatives to send their dearly departed to Joanne's funeral parlour. She felt better. There were occasional natural deaths, so her focus was to convince relatives to use Joanne's service well before the day they were needed.

Over the next week, Veronica weaned Eunice off the hooch and on to whisky, then off whisky and on to cocoa before bed. It didn't give her a headache in the morning, she remembered who she was before lunchtime, it didn't make her legs go wobbly, and it was considerably cheaper than whisky.

In under a month, Eunice had recovered from many of her symptoms and had a new lease of life. She washed herself, dressed herself, fed herself, and even went for little walks. She became stronger every day.

The time eventually came when she was able to move to a warden-assisted home and live quite independently.

While making her way down the corridor to the entrance hall, she pushed a small present into Veronica's hand. "A little thank you from me." Eunice whispered to Veronica that it was funny that Denis no longer visited her, and then she smiled and winked.

"Yes, funny that, however, you'll have a whole new set of friends soon." Veronica waved her off in a taxi, was sad to see her go, and smiled at her naughtiness. She hoped she would have as much spirit as Eunice when she reached her age.

Veronica worried that Joanne was going to go nuts when she found out that Eunice had recovered, but the present might be worth something. The small present was a Victorian brooch that Veronica immediately took to a jeweller.

"The diamonds in the surround are only small and probably came from another piece of jewellery. The clasp is nine carat gold, very worn, and the stone in the centre is a large double star sapphire. Probably late eighteen hundreds, probably Austrian originally, going by some of the filigree. Hmm. Any provenance?" asked the jeweller.

"None that I'm aware of," answered Veronica. "What would you value it at?"

"Value? Very difficult to say. Probably about £9,000 at the right auction, but on a good day, and with the right provenance, it might even fetch double that."

Veronica needed to sit down.

10

Joanne held her head in her hands, in her typical business pose, trying to fathom out how a profitable business only twelve months previously was now teetering on financial failure.

As an accountant in the past, she had spent hours, no, days, looking for a missing penny. She believed if the accounts were a penny out then the whole system was in doubt. One penny missing rang warning bells for her. Not understanding where the money was going against the income was her worst nightmare.

How there could be such a mess in the accounting processes was beyond her belief, especially when the previous owner, her Gordon, had been such a stickler for accuracy and procedures. He had been a complete pain in the arse when they had lived together, with his routines and pernickety demand for accuracy.

She sat at Gordon's desk and looked about. There were the usual certificates of merit for the funeral parlour and some faded, sepia photos of black horses with black plumes on their heads pulling a black glass carriage of yesteryear, surrounded by sombre gentlemen in tall hats, all posing with the same expression.

There were also some old photos from when Gordon was in the Army; he looked really handsome in khaki, she had to say. There was a smell of smoke when she opened one of the drawers; that sweet-smelling fashionable tobacco smoked only with a pipe.

It was obvious that, as managing director of the funeral parlour, Gordon had maintained a clear desk policy. It was probably to impress the clients and give the air of order and tranquillity necessary to support the calm of his business.

Joanne wondered how he could maintain such a policy. She soon found out. He could maintain a clear desk policy because the other drawers in his enormous desk were all stuffed full of invoices, receipts and unopened final demands. Was this the real Gordon, or was the real Gordon the one she had lived with? She really didn't understand.

Drawer by drawer she waded through the paper. Days it took her, yet still she was no further forward. She threw nothing away. Then she started on the cupboards in his office. As she opened each one the debris of paper spilled onto the floor. More sorting uncovered absolutely nothing.

Her conversations with Elsie confused her even more. Elsie looked after the embalming side of things, and the preparations of her guests, as she liked to call them. It was the side of the business Joanne had absolutely no intention of getting involved in. Elsie was often busy around the parlour in white abattoir wellies, a red rubber apron which hung down to the floor, and long, red, rubber gloves.

She explained, when questioned, that Mr Gordon did all the paper work and she looked after the guests.

"Well, who are the accountants?" asked Joanne.

"No idea. I just look after the guests," Elsie said proudly.

"Who are the auditors then?"

"No idea. Sorry, I just look after the guests."

"Well, surely you know who our solicitors are?"

"No, sorry, I just-"

"I know, I know, you just look after the guests," Joanne interrupted.

"I do more than just look after the guests, actually," said Elsie, with great pride in her voice. "I like to keep up to date so I read a lot about all the modern techniques of looking after guests. I am regularly updating our procedures from funeral parlour magazines and books."

Joanne was surprisingly impressed. "Such as?"

"For instance, I recently read a book written by an American author about his family's five generations of morticians. He made several recommendations. I found them absolutely fascinating."

"Give me an example of what you've changed."

"Well, this very learned man, because he wrote books on it, advised all morticians and funeral directors to tie the shoelaces together of guests who are to be buried. Not cremated, just buried."

"Why on earth would you do that?"

"Well, he wrote that if there is an apocalypse and all the dead rise up as zombies, the result will be hilarious. It's in black and white so it must be true! I do it now every time, as a matter of course."

Joanne resisted banging her head on the desk while whispering to herself, "You bastard, Gordon, you bastard."

There was a pause before Elsie continued. "And don't forget the sandwiches."

Joanne looked confused. "Sandwiches? What sandwiches?"

"The sandwiches the clients have at wakes."

"What are you talking about, Elsie?"

"The sandwiches. Every wake has to have sandwiches. It wouldn't be a proper wake without sandwiches, would it?"

"What?" asked Joanne, dumbfounded. "You do the embalming and then make the sandwiches for the wake?"

"No, silly. Oh, you are a one." With that, Elsie settled down in the chair opposite Joanne to chat, still wearing her rubber apron and gloves.

Joanne breathed a sigh of relief, imagining Elsie in the same rubber gloves and long apron spreading butter on to a sliced brown loaf and chopping up Spam and tomatoes.

"Not just sandwiches," Elsie clarified. "They don't just want sandwiches. That would be too boring. I do all the sausage rolls, cheese and pineapple chunks on cocktail sticks, and different 'volley vont dooferies', as Mr Gordon always called them, with different fillings inside them, and anything else fancy the clients want."

Joanne's stomach lurched. She shook her head in disbelief.

"Are you hungry? Do you want me to make you a sandwich now?"

"Thank you, Elsie, no. I'm on a diet."

"Coffee?"

"No, thanks. I think I'll have a can of pop instead."

"Well, if you're ever hungry you only have to ask and I'll drop what I'm doing and knock a sandwich up for you, quick as a flash."

"Thanks," Joanne said, without feeling. "Where's Vincent?"

"Probably in the garage polishing his baby, or out collecting."

"Collecting? Collecting what?"

"The Club money - it's Friday."

The conversation with Elsie, lovely as she was, had been draining to say the least, so Joanne thanked her and said they would chat again later.

Now, her Gordon had said that Vincent had been his right-hand man. Vincent managed the casket bearers, dealt with the funeral parlour suppliers, and oiled any other wheels of business that needed oiling.

However, Joanne hadn't seen any oiling of any business wheels for her yet! Where is his contract of employment? she wondered. Where is Elsie's too, for that matter? Filed in the invisible fairy filing cabinet, along with all the other funeral parlour legal documents, like health and safety practices and HR policies? What exactly is Vincent's job? she asked herself.

She went into the garage to find him and, sure enough, there he was polishing the big, ancient hearse. When confronted about what he did at the funeral parlour he explained that he looked after the old hearse, kept it shiny, and undertook all the vehicle maintenance himself. Then there was silence.

"Is that it?"

"Well, yes."

"What do you do on the day of a funeral?"

"Oh right, I understand now. I am the main pallbearer and I arrange the part-time casket bearers, each of whom needs to display the reverential stoop of men who have borne the best of men and women on their shoulders during their careers."

He went on to explain that his team of casket bearers had been carefully chosen for their strength and the height of their shoulders. These men were hard to find.

Their shoulder heights had to be exact, he continued. It was an art form. Where there were discrepancies in shoulder heights their shoes had to be adjusted. It was easy when one casket bearer was a bit shorter than the rest.

Vincent explained, at great length, that in his workshop he could build up any short casket bearer's shoes. However, when one was too tall it gave him a bigger problem because he then had to build up the shoes of the other three or, in the case of a very heavy client, five other pairs of shoes. And if one of them went sick, well, the problems were endless.

He added that he couldn't have anyone with a limp in his team as it would look as if the casket was on a roller coaster, and this funeral parlour was a professional parlour where folk demanded very high standards.

Joanne yawned out loud. She wanted to jump out of the window. "Tell me, Vincent, you were close to Gordon...how did he pay the suppliers?"

"Every quarter day, Miss Joanne. Never missed, even when he was poorly. They all met in the Nag's Head, on the high street, for lunch and he paid them all, every penny. Honest as the day is long was Mr Gordon. I won't have a word said against him."

To Joanne, who was used to the latest accounting techniques, what Vincent had just explained at length was a medieval practice. Quarter days? Who still used quarter days?

"What about small payments like heating or milk or petrol?"

"Ah, well, that was a bit different." There was a hesitation in Vincent's voice and Joanne pounced.

"Well?"

"Seeing as you're the boss now, Miss Joanne, I'll tell you. If they couldn't wait for the quarter day then, generous to a fault, Mr Gordon would pay with The Club money."

This was the second reference to The Club money in one day, so Joanne decided to press Vincent further. She soon wished she hadn't.

"Well, Miss, it all started in Mr Gordon's father's era, years and years ago, when I was just an apprentice here. I'll tell you how it worked."

Joanne groaned and put her head in her hands.

"He set up a club, which he called The Club. The Club was a means by which poor folk, who couldn't pay for a funeral if it came around unannounced, could save money over the years. In the early days it was a penny a week - that's an old penny, mind you - but it went up little by little and now I collect £1 a week. Then folk don't have to worry so much when the inevitable happens. Club members put their money in an envelope every week with their name on it. Like Sidney, or George, or Lillian, or Isobelle. When we get them here all their envelopes are kept together in a pile."

"What on earth has this got to do with paying the milk bill?"

"Well, I'll tell you. If Mr Gordon needed to pay someone in a hurry he went to the big fridge, where we used to keep our guests when there were too many of them for the small fridge, and took out some of The Club money."

"So, he raided The Club money to pay the milk bill?"

"Yes. That's it. You've got it."

"And you keep The Club money in the big fridge? How many people pay into The Club?"

"Most folk around here. At its height Mr Gordon's father had about four people out selling the idea and going from door to door. There were many hundreds in the beginning, but now there aren't so many, probably about three hundred."

"Three hundred people! You must be joking. You go around and collect £1 from three hundred people every Friday?"

"No, no, most drop it in once a month now, in cash, in an envelope with their name on it, just like I said. Some drop it in once a year. I just collect from about thirty folk now, once a week. I do it every Friday. Always cash, never a cheque."

That figures, thought Joanne, for there had been no record

of any such payments recorded in any of the documentation she had so painfully ploughed through.

"How much is in the big fridge, then?" she asked.

"There must be thousands of envelopes in there. Most of the early members are dead now, and because nobody knew they had been paying into The Club for years their families just paid out again. Other folk have been paying in for donkey's years and will probably outlive all of us."

Joanne wondered if she might regret looking in the big fridge, however, curiosity won her over. She and Vincent walked to the part of the funeral parlour she had so far avoided.

The big fridge wasn't locked, but as Vincent opened the heavily insulated door it creaked a warning. The swinging, single, dusty light threw shadows all about the walls, and the musty smell of disintegrating paper pervaded the long, windowless room.

Inside, there were three shelves on each side, each shelf the depth, length and height to take a single casket. The big fridge went back about four casket lengths.

However, Joanne couldn't really see them for stacked high on every shelf, on both sides, were envelopes of every shape and size. At the back of the fridge, many of the stacks of envelopes had collapsed and were all over the floor. She estimated the pile of envelopes was about four feet deep.

Leaning down, she picked up a dusty envelope which had *Emma* faintly written on it in pen. "Who's Emma?"

"No idea, long before my time," said Vincent.

The glue on the envelope had long since dried out and

Joanne carefully opened it. Four large coins slid into her hand. "What are these?"

"They're half crowns, Miss. Four of them would make up ten shillings, which in today's money is fifty pence. The dates are on the coins; it will give us an idea."

The coins were dated from the 1930s and 1940s.

"But there must be about fifty years of envelopes in here in that case."

"About that, yes, Miss."

Joanne reversed back towards the door and picked up a more recent envelope. A £20 note was poking out. It was a modern note and on the envelope was the name *Louise* in black ink. "Who's Louise?"

"Oh, that's Mrs Louise Trollop. Louise lives at 16 The Terrace, near the old bakery that closed down."

"How do you know that?"

"Because I collect from her every four months. Here's her pile of envelopes."

Sure enough, under the envelope Joanne had selected, was a pile of other envelopes, all with the name *Louise* written on the front.

"But how am I expected to know that?" she asked Vincent.

"You just ask me."

"What happens if you're not here?"

"I'm always here."

"What happens if someone who says they have been paying

in for years has a close relative die and wants to use their Club money?"

"Well, Mr Gordon used to have a long chat with them to gain their confidence, and then leave them in the office for a while saying he was going to check their account. What he actually did was to go and have a cup of tea with Elsie to give the impression of being thorough. When he came back, he would say something like, 'Well, Mrs Bloggs, you have a tidy sum in your account I have to admit. You've been very thrifty but unfortunately the price of funerals, like everything else, has gone up and up, and to do what you want to do to bury your husband in the style he deserves will be an extra £285.' Mr Gordon relied on the fact that most Club members never kept records. The vast number of Club members died before they claimed any money, and now their money just sits there gathering dust."

Joanne was dumbfounded at such a system and shook her head in disbelief. She left the big fridge, saying to Vincent, "I need a drink. And lock that door!"

11

As always, Joanne and Veronica met every Saturday evening for a meal and a catch up.

"So far," Joanne started, "you haven't sent me any business in the way we planned, but we have had £1,500 each from your first patient, and we'll get half of £9,000 each from your latest conquest."

"And I've saved two lives."

"Yes, yes, yes," Joanne dismissed the comment, "and, with some serious savings, I will break even in the funeral parlour at the end of this month, if I'm lucky."

"Well done."

"By the way, don't eat any of Elsie's sandwiches."

"Why not?"

"Just don't eat the sandwiches, OK?"

"But I like sandwiches."

"Trust me. Don't eat the sandwiches."

"OK, OK, OK, whatever," said Veronica, shrugging.

"Anyway, I have something to show you. Follow me."

"I'm not going to any embalming room, or anywhere else in this funeral parlour where there are bodies. It's creepy enough sleeping upstairs in my flat here."

"Shut up and prepare to be amazed." With that, Joanne unlocked the big fridge door and switched on the dim light. "There," she announced.

The inquisitive Veronica couldn't make out what she was looking at, then she picked up an envelope near the door and out fell a £50 note. On the outside of the plain envelope was the name *Doris*. "Who's Doris?" she asked.

"No idea." Joanne then went through the whole saga of The Club, as explained previously by Vincent, and watched Veronica's jaw drop lower and lower.

"There must be thousands and thousands of pounds in cash here!" she exclaimed as she moved further down the big fridge, opening some of the older envelopes and examining some of the coins. She explained that some of the coins could be much more valuable than their face value, which was a dimension that hadn't occurred to Joanne.

Veronica slowly started to understand the situation and, after some deliberation, went on to say that if they drew a line in the big fridge where those people who were currently contributing finished, then they could reasonably assume that anyone further back in the fridge was dead and never going to claim their Club money.

"We could help ourselves!" she declared.

"That's exactly what Gordon was doing. That's why there are

no accounts. That's one of the reasons why everything was paid in cash."

Over the next three hours, the two of them brought out a selection of envelopes from the back of the fridge. They put them in name order, if the names were still legible, and added up the amounts.

The largest number of envelopes was about three hundred from one woman. They started with a single penny in each envelope and went up to two shillings and sixpence a week. But there were heaps and heaps of coins that were loose on the floor where the envelopes had fallen apart.

Veronica was excited when she saw a cartwheel two pence piece. She went on to identify ship-halfpennies, bun-pennies, three-penny bits, sixpences, florins and half-crowns; all a foreign language to Joanne.

"How do you know about all this coin stuff?"

"My dad's a numismatist."

"I never knew that," said Joanne.

"He's been doing it for years and years. I could ask him to value some of the older coins, if you like. We are talking of a lot of money here, Jo Jo. Does this mean I can stop working in the care home?"

"Certainly not. We don't want to arouse any suspicions at this point. The only reason I said we would look at the older coins is that Vincent never goes to the back of the big fridge, so he wouldn't notice if some went missing."

"It doesn't matter, they all belong to you now," said Veronica.

"Yes, you're right, I suppose they do."

At the end of the evening, they put the coins and older envelopes in ice cream cartons, and bags and boxes. In fact, they put them in any containers they could find.

It was long past midnight when they at last sat down for the final drink of the night.

Veronica spotted Joanne fingering a shiny new ring on her right hand, and asked her about it.

"Oh, this thing? It's nothing, just something a lady who came here wanted me to have."

"Let's have a look. Wow!" The ring was a solitaire diamond, and a big one. "She just gave it to you? I wish someone would just give me a solitaire diamond ring. In fact, any ring would do."

Veronica could see that Joanne was being very coy. She sensed she had found some high ground; a place she experienced rarely with Joanne so she pressed the point, enjoying her discomfort. "What did the lady say?"

"She was very poorly at the time and didn't have long to live. I was arranging her own funeral with her, you know, all the hymns and flowers and the arrangements for her wake, and so on. It was all very sad. She died four weeks ago and we buried her a week later. But, during the meeting about her arrangements, out of the blue, she produced a wad of £1,000 in notes and said, 'Please use all this money to get a really nice stone.' So here it is."

And with that, once again, a slightly guilty Joanne splayed out her fingers, displaying the sparkling ring on her finger to a speechless Veronica.

12

The night shifts came and went for Veronica; same old, same old. One evening, she was instructed to come in early the next day and report to the care home manager.

Her mind flicked back over all the things she had done wrong over the last few weeks: the days she left a bit early, the shifts she hadn't cleaned up at the end of properly, and some of her night shift entries were a bit sparse, to say the least.

Then her mind moved onto more serious stuff. Had Denis reported her? He would have to be pretty sure to avoid the Samoan whisky issue, but her comment that, "The other nurses here will beat seven bells out of you!" sprung to mind. She really must curb her righteous indignation.

Or had George's daughter told the care home manager about the £5,000 cheque?

Veronica revisited the exact same feelings she had experienced many times as she had stood outside her headmistress's study door. She remembered in those days that headmistress's summonses had been a very effective laxative, and today was no different. Veronica knocked and waited.

The conversation, however, had nothing to do with any misdemeanours. In fact, it was quite the reverse. She was asked if she would like to look after one of the owners of the care home who needed twenty four hour care. Veronica was a bit taken aback. This wasn't how most of her summonses by authority ended.

Veronica asked what was wrong with the owner who needed twenty four hour care, and was told she had fallen down some concrete steps two years previously, and fractured her leg in several places. Her leg was so distorted the hospital needed to use steel rods and many pins. It was thought she picked up an infection from one of the rods or screws. Her leg went from bad to worse and eventually had to be amputated. The amputation then went horribly wrong and she developed gangrene.

Veronica winced as the dreadful account unfolded. Following the discussion covering the list of her duties, Veronica said she would probably agree to the new position but would like to meet the lady first.

Together, she and the manager walked to a part of the house she had never been to before. As soon as the bedroom door was opened, the smell of rotting flesh hit Veronica like a brick.

She was introduced to Mrs Charlotte Ann Wendover, who had lived in the house all her fifty seven years. Veronica instantly warmed to her. The care home manager then suggested Veronica stay whilst she dressed the leg.

The bandages came off slowly, revealing a terrible wound oozing with pus and discharge. Charlotte Ann, who preferred to be called Miss Tan from her Sunday school teacher days in the local church, when the kids had found her full name a bit of a mouthful, flinched as the bandages were unwound. The pain in her face was real and the care home manager was careful and gentle; a side Veronica hadn't seen previously.

At the end of the application of ointment and redressing operation, the exhausted old lady flopped back onto her pillows and was soon fast asleep. They crept out of her room and disposed of the evil smelling bandages, before walking to the manager's office for a cup of tea.

Veronica was slowly changing her mind about the manager. She had seen a caring side to her for the first time, and was disappointed with herself that she had jumped to a number of premature assumptions.

The manager explained there were actually two owners of the Bethesda Care Home - sisters who had lived in the lovely house all their lives. However, they were diametrically opposite in nature.

"If you ask me, their fathers came from stables at opposite ends of the village to be so dissimilar, if you get what I mean," whispered the manager. "The elder sister is Miss Violet Ann Mainwaring, who insists on being called Miss Violet Ann. The staff all call her Miss Violent Ann."

"Where does Miss Violet Ann live?"

"Here, in another part of the house, near to Miss Tan. She also has care but doesn't need it as much as her sister. Miss Violent Ann has an evil tongue, the patience of a rattlesnake, is as snappy as a crocodile with toothache, and hates everyone. She's the reason most carers leave, so we've set up a specific team to look after her. She used to fire staff for the slightest things. I'll give you an example.

A lovely, well-trained nurse joined our team some months ago. She made breakfast and took it in to Miss Violent Ann at exactly 8.00 am on the dot, as instructed. She wasn't to know that Miss Violent Ann doesn't like brown eggs because she thinks they are white eggs that still have poo on them. She has had this thing about them since she was a child.

Rather than explain and let the young nurse get some more, she threw the whole tray back at her. The eggs and toast and tea went all over her uniform. The young nurse never came back. Miss Violent Ann can be really spiteful."

"I wish you hadn't told me her nickname. I'm sure I'll use it if I see her."

"You'll be OK, she's a bit deaf."

"What about Miss Tan's temper?"

"She hasn't an unkind bone in her body. Not one. She is a sweet lady, and thanks me every time I dress her leg, despite how much it hurts."

"Thank goodness for that. When do I start?"

"Tonight. I've dressed it now, but by the morning it will need dressing again. Please look after Miss Tan as she's quite special to us all, and won't be with us long. Six to nine months at the most."

Time went by and Miss Tan and Veronica struck up a friendship. Laughter came from her room for the first time in ages, and each looked forward to the other's company.

Veronica and Miss Tan talked about everything and nothing. Sometimes a whole night passed and they were still chatting when Veronica had to prepare breakfast. To Miss Tan, Veronica was a tonic. To Veronica, Miss Tan was the best patient she had ever had the good fortune to nurse.

Veronica asked Miss Tan about her life in a stately home, when she and her sister were children, and was mesmerised by stories of playing in the grounds and Christmas parties. There were always questions from Veronica.

When Miss Tan was recounting her time as a Sunday school teacher, Veronica asked, "Didn't you ever get fed up with the little ones?"

"No, never. They were all lovely and each was a little person in their own right. You could see the makings of their character and humour even at that early age. I was helping to mould their thinking. What a privilege. Now and again the odd little boy or girl would be a bit naughty, but it never lasted for long."

"I think I would be inclined to wait until the vicar wasn't looking and give the little treasure an encouraging, corrective clip!"

"Goodness! I couldn't have done that. They were all delightful, every one of them. I can still remember the names of the really good children, and also the names of, let's call the others, the more adventurous children."

"And you did this every Sunday, week in, week out? You were a real hero. It was cheap babysitting for the parents wasn't it?"

"I didn't see it like that and I loved every minute of it. However, there was one thing I really didn't like doing."

"Which was?" asked Veronica.

"I hated tying wet shoe laces on a dry day!"

There was a pause while Veronica visualised the situation, then the two of them couldn't stop laughing. Veronica had to shush Miss Tan to prevent her waking the other residents.

Veronica often dressed her wound three times in a night, to make her more comfortable, if it was giving her trouble. When the pain became too much for Miss Tan to bear, Veronica would sit for hours and just rub her back, and recount tales of her holidays with Joanne, to take her mind off things.

Veronica knew the morphine would start to lose its effect one day. Here was one lovely lady for whom Veronica couldn't do enough.

One night, when she went into Miss Tan's room, there was a distinguished gentleman sitting by the side of her bed. He was close enough to hold her frail hand in one of his hands, and close the other over it in a protective manner.

Veronica had to hold back her tongue, for the gentleman was the spitting image of Joanne's late husband, Gordon.

"Veronica, this is Godfrey Wendover, my husband. We've been together now for thirty five years, barring the war years, and I love him very much. He's with me as soon as you leave, and stays with me all night when you can't."

There had been signs that someone else had been in Miss Tan's room sometimes, but Veronica assumed it had been Miss Violet Ann. "I'm very pleased to meet you," she said, shaking Godfrey's hand.

"The reason I'm telling you now is because your cousin

Joanne, who is running the funeral parlour in the town, will soon end up in a lot of trouble if you don't warn her," divulged Miss Tan.

"Warn her? Warn her about what?" The phrase 'warn her' immediately captured Veronica's attention.

Well, I'll tell you. Godfrey here," Miss Tan said, patting his hand affectionately, "used to run it."

"But I thought that...I thought that Gordon, Joanne's husband, ran the funeral parlour. I'm confused," Veronica stuttered, shaking her head, not understanding anything so far.

"I'll start at the beginning with the Wendover family, so you know all the background." With that, she gave Godfrey's hand a squeeze and smiled a melting smile at him. He returned the smile and Veronica knew this pair were still deeply in love.

"Gordon and Godfrey were brothers," began Miss Tan. "In fact, they were more than just brothers, they were twin brothers, and their father, old man Wendover, ran the funeral parlour in the town for about thirty years before the war. It was a very popular funeral parlour and did very well.

When war broke out in 1939, the brothers were eighteen and both of them decided to go and fight for England. Before Godfrey went off to fight, he and I eloped and were married.

All hell was let loose in my family because we'd eloped. My father refused to speak to me for days, my mother had apoplexy and wouldn't come out of her bedroom for a week, and my sister, Violet Ann, was just so jealous you could see a green aura all around her for months." Miss Tan's eyes twinkled with the telling of the story.

"You have to remember that things were much more sober and conventional in those days, not as they are now with rampant promiscuity, and one parent families, and the like. We were breaking the traditional family mould and, oh, how I loved it! I also believed unfalteringly that Godfrey would come home to me after the war and if he didn't, and we only had one day together, then I wanted to have spent that one special day with him as husband and wife. And I would do it all over again."

There was another smile, another squeeze of the hand. "We were so young but so in love."

"It still shows," Veronica said, with feeling.

"You met Gordon Wendover, didn't you?" Miss Tan confirmed.

"Yes, I did. I went around a few times for a meal at Joanne and Gordon's place. When I first saw you, Godfrey, I thought you were Gordon Wendover as you're so alike, or, sorry, were so alike. However, there the similarity ends for Gordon nearly drove me nuts! I couldn't take to him at all, with all his systems and routines. What Joanne saw in him was beyond me. He was pedantic, pernickety, arcane, and very deep."

Godfrey listened, nodding in agreement.

Veronica quickly rewound. Here was Godfrey, whose twin brother Gordon had recently died, patiently listening to her rabbiting on, berating his dead brother. "Oh, I'm so sorry Godfrey, my insensitive mouth sometimes outpaces my brain. I shouldn't have said any of that. I'm sure Gordon had loads of good points too."

"It's alright, it's fine," said Godfrey resignedly. "It's how we all felt about him."

Miss Tan continued with the tale that was to hold Veronica's attention to the last word.

"Well, where was I? Oh yes, it was 1939 and Gordon was far more sensible than Godfrey, as you would expect. Even though Gordon had several women admirers throwing themselves at him, he decided to delay any thoughts of courtship or marriage until he returned home. He said he needed to concentrate on his survival. Women would be a distraction. Out of sync with his life plan. Gordon wouldn't let anybody interfere with his life plan, would he Godfrey?" Miss Tan asked the question with more than a hint of sarcasm.

"No, he wouldn't. There was a level of arrogance in Gordon that even I couldn't fathom," confirmed Godfrey. Even though he was my brother, I thought him a complete pain in the arse."

"Godfrey!" admonished Miss Tan.

"Sorry."

Miss Tan continued. "Gordon and Godfrey joined the same regiment, but in different units. When the war was over, Gordon's unit marched through the town in triumph, with bands playing and crowds waving flags, but Godfrey's unit had been completely wiped out. The Wendover family were in mourning for weeks. Me too, although I secretly believed he would come home somehow. I just knew he would. I had an unshakable faith in Providence." She smiled at the thought.

"However, what had actually happened was that my

Godfrey and three others had survived the attack, but ended up way behind enemy lines. Their only possible option was to make their way back through occupied Europe. On the journey back, and despite travelling only at night, one by one each of his mates was killed. The first was immediately shot as a spy when he was captured, the second died of a wound that became infected, and the third died when they were attempting a river crossing at night. The current took him away and over a weir. Eventually, my brave soldier arrived on the shores of France just as peace was declared. He then managed to get a boat back home. I think he would have swum across the Channel to be with me, wouldn't you, darling?"

Godfrey smiled his confirmation, his eyes misting at the memories.

"Anyway, my Godfrey decided not to tell anyone that he had made his way home, not even the Army, for everyone at home had already grieved for him. This contrary information would have left them not knowing what to think. He worried about me too, and how I would react, and whether the shock would be too much for me. He is a darling, isn't he? Godfrey decided neither his family nor mine would believe the Army, even if they said he was still alive, so he decided to meet us all in the flesh."

Miss Tan adjusted herself gingerly against her cushions, trying to get comfortable. She waved off Veronica's offer of help, and continued the story.

"When Godfrey eventually arrived home, he went to see Gordon first to make sure everything was as he'd left it - his family, and me. Once Gordon recovered from the shock, he told Godfrey that I was the only one who wouldn't believe he was dead, and how every night I'd prayed for his safe return. However, the next thing Gordon had to tell him was that their father, old man Wendover, had died six weeks earlier. He had died of a heart attack very suddenly at his business premises - the funeral parlour."

Veronica decided all the jokes about how convenient that was were inappropriate under the circumstances.

Godfrey took up the story from Miss Tan. "Gordon told me our father had been buried in the family plot in the village churchyard four weeks before I arrived home. Father bequeathed the funeral parlour to whom he thought was his only surviving son - Gordon."

Miss Tan nodded along.

"Well, Gordon was horrified at the thought of running a funeral parlour, so he decided straight away that it was a poisoned chalice. He didn't want anything to do with the business. He'd left the old couple who worked for our father, Vincent and Elsie, to run it until he found a buyer. Gordon said he had put the word about town that he wanted to sell the funeral parlour but, up until then, nobody had come forward with an offer. He had even put the sale in the hands of an estate agent, but by the time I came home there had been no takers."

Godfrey looked at Miss Tan and she motioned for him to continue.

"After a couple of bottles of beer and some whisky at our reunion, a thought came to us at the same time. As I had no job, or any chance of a job after the war, I could run the funeral parlour posing as Gordon, and at night live here with Tan. Gordon wanted to continue running his secret little office in a nearby town, doing whatever he did, going home to his gold digging first wife, recounting the tough times he was having making ends meet with the funeral business."

Veronica was rapt by the tale. "What happened next?" she asked.

"Well, we still looked remarkably alike. Nobody would have been any the wiser, as long as we were never seen together. It was also a way of saving me from paying any Income Tax or National Insurance, and giving me a job. It also solved a problem for Gordon in the form of someone he could trust running the funeral parlour, who would squirrel away money and other things."

Godfrey took a drink from a glass of water, and refreshed his wife's.

"There was also the dilemma of my widow's pension," said Miss Tan. "My sister and I had spent every penny we had on turning our family home into the Bethesda Care Home, and my dead husband's war pension helped. It all seemed to make perfect sense at the time. Nobody ever thought to look this many years forward with the deception. It has multiplied the complications for us a hundred-fold."

"How?" asked Veronica.

"Gordon and his gold digger's marriage ended in the divorce courts. It all became very messy and cost him dearly to settle, but for some reason he hung on to the funeral parlour. I don't think it was much of a decision, for I really don't think Lady Muck wanted anything to do with it. That sort of a business was well beneath her, and she knew Gordon had been struggling to make a go of it," said Miss Tan, with a hint of contempt that Veronica was surprised to hear.

"It seems strange that a man with his intellect would fall for a devious woman. Was he her first husband?" asked Veronica.

"You're very perceptive. No, she turned out to be a serial divorcee. Gordon was her third husband in six years. Love is blind," answered Godfrey.

"And stupid!" snapped Veronica.

Miss Tan took up the story again. "Shortly after that dreadful divorce, Gordon married your cousin Joanne, despite their twenty year age difference, and made her Mrs Gordon Wendover II. They seemed happy until his unfortunate bath night. It was sad enough that Gordon was dead but Godfrey, who had been running the funeral parlour for years and years posing as Gordon, had to disappear immediately as well. To all intents and purposes, he was dead!"

Miss Tan paused for another sip of water, helped by Godfrey. While she sipped the water, he tried to lighten the seriousness of the situation. "Gordon's first wife was not a nice person at all. She was a bit like a grenade. As soon as she removed the ring his whole house was gone!"

Miss Tan smiled and restarted her explanation. "Why am I sharing all this with you Veronica? Well, I'll tell you. You have been very kind to me and never once winced at the awful sight of my leg. Nothing has been too much trouble for you, and you have made my last few weeks bearable. I like you very much, Veronica. However, your cousin, Mrs Joanne Wendover, Godfrey's sister-in-law, is soon going to be in serious trouble. I owe you a huge debt of gratitude so, in some sort of repayment, you need to warn her. You must promise us that this conversation has to be in the strictest of confidence."

Veronica nodded her agreement, thinking there might be some unpaid debts on the business, or some administration issues. Nothing could have prepared her for what came next.

"The funeral parlour that Joanne is looking after never made any real money, and probably never will. It's a front for what was Gordon's other business."

"His secret out of town business?" asked Veronica, who was struggling to keep up.

"Yes."

"Which is?"

"Money laundering."

"What? Money laundering? Joanne's business is a front for money laundering?" Veronica laughed out loud. "Never in a million years! She says the administration of the funeral parlour is a shambles - sorry, Godfrey - and the financial systems are still in the middle ages, but here's no way money laundering could be taking place. She would have spotted it. Surely, to launder money he would have needed sophisticated systems, multiple bank accounts, fancy contacts abroad, hit men, and goodness only knows what else?" queried Veronica, unable to contemplate Joanne not having spotted even a hint of deception.

"Trust me, it really is a front for money laundering," Miss Tan said sternly, trying to demonstrate the seriousness of the situation. "Joanne will very likely get caught up in what's happening by default. We believe you are very fond of her and won't want her getting caught."

"Fond is stretching it a bit. We're more like good friends," joked Veronica, but immediately became serious again. "Why tell me now?"

"Because she has a shipment due in next Wednesday night."

"A shipment? Wednesday? Oh no, this doesn't sound good. A shipment of what? Money? Why have I become nervous all of a sudden? This doesn't sound good at all. Joanne's going to have a fit!"

Veronica rose from her chair and walked around the room, trying to clear her head. After a few moments she suggested a way out of the dilemma. "But surely all she has to do is be honest. She's just taken over the business. She's completely innocent. All she has to do is claim she knows nothing about any of it."

"Sorry, but it might not be as simple as that," answered Miss Tan. "We've thought about this a lot, haven't we Godfrey? We believe this is how it would look to the authorities."

She held her thumb up in the air. "Number one. Joanne's husband, Gordon Wendover, leaves his money laundering business to his newly acquired young, accountant wife, Joanne, in his will, then dies suddenly in the bath. Improbable. She says she doesn't know anything about his business interests. Implausible."

Her index finger joined her thumb. "Number two. If Gordon Wendover hasn't been running the funeral parlour for years, then who has? If my Godfrey's deception is discovered then it will soon follow that he hasn't paid any Income Tax or National Insurance contributions since the war some thirty five years ago. He will go to prison for a long time and I just couldn't live without him. It would be a disaster for us."

Miss Tan's middle finger extended. "Number three. Would Elsie or Vincent, under pressure, be able to stick to the story that they don't know anything about money laundering? Very doubtful. If they did break, they would both be heavily implicated. Their financial circumstances would be investigated with a fine tooth comb, and their house would be searched from top to bottom, where a considerable amount of cash would be uncovered. Godfrey warned them not to keep so much money in the house, but Vincent said they couldn't put it in a bank because it would look suspicious. They did put the maximum amount in premium bonds, but there was still lots left over."

Godfrey shrugged his shoulder asking, "What else could I have done?"

Miss Tan continued, "An automatic custodial sentence for each would follow as accessories to the serious crime of money laundering." She held up a fourth finger, along with the others. "Number four. If Elsie or Vincent broke, their story would also lead the police to me, and the fact that I'm not a widow at all. I owe thousands upon thousands of pounds for illegally collecting my widow's war pension for years. If I go to prison, I wouldn't last a night without Godfrey. It's unthinkable."

There were genuine tears in Miss Tan's eyes as she set out the problems for Veronica. She dropped her hand back to her lap as an anxious Godfrey tidied some silver hair from her face.

After a long pause Veronica broke the silence. "How does it work then?" she asked, unable to comprehend the story that had just unfolded. There were so many questions buzzing around her head, with no answers forthcoming.

Miss Tan wiped the tears from her eyes and continued. "Well, when someone on a cruise ship dies at sea, arrangements are made for their body to be repatriated. All the paper work is organised by the cruise ship doctor, and it accompanies the casket like a passport on its homeward journey. The body can't stay on board the ship in the port; it has to be taken to a registered, safe funeral parlour. Old man Wendover secured the bona fide contract to accept these caskets many years ago on the south coast, and the funeral parlour has renewed the contract every year since. The casket is kept in the secure little fridge at the funeral parlour, until arrangements are made for Vincent, the hearse driver, to transport the casket and the deceased to their UK hometown, or onward if their home is abroad."

Miss Tan was waning with the stress of explaining the process so Veronica held her shaky hand while she took another sip of water.

She insisted on continuing. "The money laundering scheme uses the exact same procedure, only there's no body in the casket. The body is a bandaged dummy, stuffed full of money. As Gordon's father had been doing this for years using a genuinely signed contract with all the shipping companies, the authorities never asked any questions. In truth, there were only very occasional calls for this genuine service."

"What happens when the casket is in Joanne's funeral parlour?"

"Godfrey, please will you tell the rest of the story? I'm getting so tired."

Godfrey stroked his wife's hand and took up the tale. "We,

that's Vincent and me, open the casket and take out the head that's covered in bandages."

"Arrgghh! What, you rip off the head? Oh, that's gross. What about the smell? What about all the blood, and steak and kidney, and goo, and stuff?" asked Veronica, turning pale.

"It's all right, there's not a real body in the casket, remember? It's just a body shape of stiff bandages. The head is our cut of the money. I think others have an arm, or a leg, and the body is the bit that ends up at the destinations. We fill the empty head with paper, put it back in place, tidy it all up, and screw the lid back on. It's always delivered to us at night by men wearing sunglasses, in a hearse with darkened windows. There's always a note to identify the next destination in amongst our share of the money. Vincent then drives the casket to wherever it needs to go next. Maybe a ship at Harwich, maybe a big house in the Lake District, it could be anywhere, but it's always a different place. The next delivery will be on Wednesday night and it's Saturday today. Do you realise now why you need to warn her?"

'Oh yes," said a very unsteady Veronica, standing up. "I'm sure Joanne will be really grateful for being tipped off, but she's not going to like this. She's not going to like this one bit. She's going to be apoplectic with Gordon when she hears about this. She's really working her tail off to formalise things, sort out the admin, and make it into a paying business. It's really going to hit the fan when she hears. I'd better make some tea."

13

On Sunday night, Veronica poured Joanne a very large drink and then poured herself an even larger one. She passed Joanne the drink. "You're going to need this."

A slightly startled Joanne snapped a few questions. "Why? What have you done now? You're not in trouble, are you? Has someone found out about our plan? You haven't lost your job, again have you? Has that Denis come back?"

"Shut up, Jo Jo, and sit down. This is really serious stuff."

"Oh, here we go again. I knew I should have been the one who went to the care home and it's only because you're such a squeamish soul that I let you talk me into this idea in the first place."

"Hold on a minute," said Veronica. "First of all, it was your plan and second of all, this has nothing to do with the care home. It's about your funeral parlour, so stop talking for a while and just listen."

Veronica sat opposite Joanne and looked her straight in the eye, not slouched on the settee as normal. Now she had

Joanne's full attention - this was serious and Joanne had the message loud and clear. Veronica never sounded like this.

"Gordon's twin brother, Godfrey, who I met last night for the first time, has been running the funeral parlour posing as Gordon for decades," she announced quickly, relieved to have said it.

"What? I didn't even know he had-"

"Shhh. I'll answer all your questions when I've taken you through the whole story. Please just pay attention, it's really complicated."

Veronica took a swig of Dutch courage. "Godfrey Wendover, that's your Gordon's twin brother, is still alive but completely stateless. He was supposed to have been killed in the war when his whole unit was wiped out, but he never declared to the Army that he was OK when he returned home safe and sound."

"How did he get away with that?"

"Shhh. Godfrey Wendover married Miss Tan before he went to war. She's the lady I care for I told you all about, and she owns half of the Bethesda Care Home. Gordon Wendover, that's your real husband, never ever worked at the funeral parlour. He wanted to sell it as soon as it was bequeathed to him by his father. That's why you were so confused about the accounts being in such a mess. Gordon couldn't cope with the shambles of how his father used to manage the business; the disorder was just too much for him. Are you following?"

Joanne nodded.

"So, the two brothers devised a plan. Firstly, to give Godfrey a job, but because he wasn't a real person it meant he didn't need to pay any National Insurance or Income Tax. Secondly, Gordon trusted Godfrey to keep the funeral parlour running as a front for Gordon's undercover job of money laundering, and other things."

"What? My Gordon's real job was money laundering? You must be joking. My Gordon? Money laundering? Never in a million years. He couldn't, he wouldn't-"

"Shut up, Jo Jo. You must listen because now it involves you. Yes, money laundering. Gordon was into money laundering in a big way. Just listen. A casket, supposedly carrying a dead passenger from a cruise ship, is delivered here at night. Vincent and Godfrey open the coffin and take off the head. It's just a mould of stiff bandages, like a mummy. They empty out the cash, tidy the head up, fill it with paper, and put the mummy back together. Then they screw the lid back on to the casket and Vincent drives it to its next destination. Your funeral parlour is just one of the destinations the dodgy cash travels to through the UK, and you get a cut."

Veronica let this part of the story sink in for a few moments before she moved on. "You don't know anything about this because there hasn't been a delivery since you took over."

"But-"

"Shhh. Will you just let me finish? You can't plead ignorance to the authorities, because no one would ever believe an experienced accountant didn't know what was happening in her husband's business. Vincent and Elsie would crack if they tried to brazen it out. They would be seen as accessories and would definitely go to jail. Godfrey will go to jail for not paying Income Tax or National Insurance for practically a hundred years, and his wife, Miss Tan, will go to jail for claiming a widow's pension for decades. In her condition she wouldn't last a night. It's all a mess and I don't know what to do."

Having finally listened to the whole process, Joanne picked up the now empty glasses and walked into her tiny kitchen. Her mood was a kaleidoscope of emotions. It explained the injections of cash at irregular intervals, but she had been focussing on looking for patterns. She knew her Gordon couldn't have tolerated chaos, so somebody else must have been involved.

Her naïve account about the transactions was that Gordon, or Godfrey, or whoever was running the funeral parlour, must have waited until they had a wad of cash and cheques, and then gone to the bank to pay them all in together at random times of the month.

But money laundering? Joanne's mind was clicking and whirring with the news as she prepared fresh drinks. Currently, the funeral parlour was breaking even, but only just. Money laundering could be a solution. It seemed to have been happening for years without a hitch, so why rock the boat? She dropped the ice in the glasses and argued back and forth with herself. Money laundering? Enormous risks, huge fines, the potential to go to prison - a completely different ball game to anything she had ever contemplated.

But very, very lucrative.

14

Vincent and Elsie sat in Joanne's office, on Monday morning, like two naughty school children. They were very nervous. All she had said was that she knew about the delivery on Wednesday night, and wanted to talk to them.

She entered the room like a headmistress, and drew up her chair. Veronica came in and sat alongside her. "You both know Veronica. She also knows all about the money laundering," said Joanne.

Vincent and Elsie looked furtively at each other.

"You can both stop worrying about Veronica. She's the one who tipped me off about Wednesday night's delivery. Now, let's not beat about the bush as we haven't the time. How does this work?"

Vincent spoke first. "Do you want to continue accepting the deliveries? You don't have to."

"I'll tell you in a minute. I haven't made up my mind yet."

"OK. Well, this is how it works. We get a call on the Wednesday afternoon to let us know the time of delivery, so if anything is wrong we can abort it. The code conversation is, 'What colour shrouds do you have in stock?' If everything is OK, we answer, 'We have white ones.' If there is any shadow of doubt then we say, 'We only have black ones at the moment.' We've only cancelled the delivery once when the local authority had dug up the road outside the funeral parlour to lay some pipes, and we couldn't even get our hearse in."

Joanne nodded.

"When the casket is delivered, there's no discussion with the driver or his colleague whatsoever. They unload and wheel the casket into our foyer, turn around, and just leave. Any attempt at conversation is met with a scowl. They get into their empty hearse and drive off. I have only heard one of them speak once, and that was when he slipped off the curb and hurt his ankle. It sounded like a European accent, but I'm really not sure. This will be the first delivery without Gordon to help, but I've been doing this for years and know exactly what to do. We unscrew the coffin lid and detach the head. Inside the head are bundles of notes - £7,000 exactly."

"£7,000?" Joanne's eyes opened wider, and Veronica started to visibly perspire.

"Yes, £7,000 in used British notes of different denominations. We stuff the empty head with London Evening Standard newspapers, rather than the local press like the Town Trumpet, so nobody can connect it with this town, and then we put the body back together. In amongst our cash is a typed address for me to deliver the casket on its onward journey. Once, while we were detaching the head the left arm was loose and we had to re-attach it. That was full of Belgium notes. We peeped inside the other arm and that was full of French notes. That same night I drive the casket to the new address. Nobody says a word.

It really does run like clockwork. I'm back by the morning, or later the next day. Gordon paid Elsie and me in the notes and then took his share. The rest went back into the business."

"What's your role in all this, Elsie?"

"Oh, I look after Vincent's back if things go wrong," she said, sounding like a gangster's moll.

Both Veronica and Joanne sat up at her comment and leaned forward. "Things go wrong? Like how?" asked Joanne.

"Well, once they brought in a real body and it had been decaying badly for some time. I had to-"

"Never mind. That's enough, thank you Elsie. We get the picture," Veronica interjected, having already gone white. "How often do you do this?" she then asked. "The normal delivery I mean, not the messy one that went wrong?"

Vincent looked over at Veronica nervously, then back at Joanne to see if it was OK to answer the question.

"I told you, she's alright. Veronica's with me."

"Nothing's regular," he said. "Sometimes we do it three times in a week, and other times we do it just once a month. I haven't heard a thing since you took over, so that's why our income figures are in a bit of a mess of late."

"Bit like sex and me," chipped in Veronica, to lighten the moment. "All or nothing."

Joanne scowled at her.

"OK, so what did Gordon pay you?" asked Joanne next, knowing Veronica could easily check the figures with

Godfrey later, which would be a measure of the pair's honesty.

"He was very generous. He paid me £1,000, Elsie £500, and he kept £2,000 for himself every time. He then paid our suppliers in cash on the quarter days in the pub, and the rest went into the bank."

Joanne remembered the strange amounts of cash that went into the bank at odd times of the month, but with no accounts it was impossible to have any sort of audit trail.

Vincent went on, "If you think Mr Gordon was being too generous then we'll both take a cut, won't we Elsie? We have so much cash sloshing about at home we don't know what to do with it all. It's in the cupboards, in the coal house, under the bed, and under the floorboards. It's becoming a bit of a worry."

"I wish I had a worry like that. If you need somewhere to keep it, I'll happily look after it for you." There was a pause. "For a percentage," said Veronica.

Joanne decided she didn't need to check the figures with Veronica. Here were two folk who seemed as loyal and honest as the day is long except, that is, for their part in money laundering, tax evasion and fraud.

"Do you and Elsie want to keep doing it?" asked Joanne.

"Definitely." They both nodded enthusiastically, looking at each other to confirm. "It's the best excitement anyone could have at our time of life," said Vincent.

"Right, let's do it!" replied Joanne assertively. "What do you want us to do on Wednesday night?"

"Nothing. Absolutely nothing. Please stay in your office until they have gone and then we'll come and get you."

"That seems fair to me," Joanne said, looking at Veronica.

"That's OK with me too," said Veronica nervously. "But don't you think we need to talk about this a little bit more, Jo Jo?"

"No, it's fine. We'll do it!"

Wednesday night came and, at the prescribed hour, a blacked out hearse drew up outside the funeral parlour.

From behind a tiny crack in the curtains of the office, Joanne and Veronica jostled each other. They watched Vincent open the garage doors, ready for the hearse to back into, then close them again once it was parked.

Inside the funeral parlour garage, the passenger door and the driver's door of the delivery hearse opened at the same time.

Out stepped two gorilla lookalikes in sunglasses and suits. They slammed the doors in unison, walked to the back of the hearse, opened the back doors, and wheeled a casket out into the reception area. Together they closed the back doors and, once back inside the hearse, slammed the driver's and passenger's doors in unison.

Vincent opened the garage doors again, and the vehicle slid silently off into the night. Once the delivery hearse was out of sight, Vincent closed the doors and turned off the outside lights.

Elsie then collected Joanne and Veronica, who were so excited they raced down the corridor to get a good look. They saw a normal enough casket, the only difference being the name of a ship was engraved on a brass plaque on the side.

Vincent started unscrewing the lid, which seemed to take ages.

"A watched pot..." Elsie reminded them.

Elsie and Vincent lifted the lid off and placed it on a trestle stand. The bandaged body then became visible. Veronica started to change colour, but Joanne couldn't wait to see the head removed.

With Elsie's help, Vincent carefully lifted the fragile head from its position, and put it onto an adjacent table. Just as they had described, it was carefully packed with bundles of mixed, used banknotes.

The notes were removed, the head stuffed with old, London Evening Standard newspapers, and then carefully replaced. The casket lid was put back in position and Vincent screwed it down.

Elsie flicked through the notes and found the new address for Vincent, which was in Harwich. She then helped wheel the trolley with the delivery casket to their old hearse.

Just as Vincent was getting into the driver's seat, Elsie shouted, "Wait!"

The three of them froze. What had she seen? Police? Had the gorillas returned? Adrenaline rushed from low down in Joanne's and Veronica's stomachs. Their eyes were everywhere, looking for the reflections of blue lights, and their ears were strained for sounds of distant sirens.

The same thought was going through their minds. Not on

their very first delivery? Surely not! They couldn't be that unlucky.

"You forgot your sandwiches," said Elsie to Vincent, affectionately passing him a bundle, and kissing him on his cheek.

Vincent thanked her and the old hearse rumbled off into the night, leaving behind a very relieved Joanne and Veronica.

The garage doors were closed, lights were turned off, and the three of them went to Joanne's office. There they counted out £7,000.

Joanne was about to count the money out into four piles, when Elsie suggested they just count it into two piles, for she and Vincent had made a decision. They thought that as this was Joanne and Veronica's first delivery, they should share it all between just them.

15

The days returned to normal, with a slightly happier Joanne running the funeral parlour and balancing the books, and Veronica insisting on staying on night shifts to care for Miss Tan.

As a candle flickers towards the end of its life, so Miss Tan's health was flickering. Morphine on demand was helping her to fade in and out of consciousness.

Godfrey hardly left her side, but wanted to hear the stories about the funeral parlour, which Veronica embellished wherever she could to make him laugh.

Godfrey, in turn, confirmed the amounts of cash that Vincent and Elsie had been paid from the deliveries, and said they had been getting exactly the same share for many years.

He couldn't speak highly enough about the old, married couple. Vincent and Elsie were the salt of the earth and, despite being in their seventies, very professional and dependable in everything they did. Godfrey described them as folk who sent out good pebble ripples.

It was a secret comfort to Veronica that Vincent and Elsie were working with Joanne, for although she had masses of business sense she had about as much customer care and empathy for clients as a dead cat! In the funeral business compassion seemed to be the difference between success and failure, especially in a small community.

Luckily for Joanne, an unexpected cold snap of harsh weather arrived, and the real funeral business started picking up. In fact, for the first time since Joanne had taken over, she started to feel busy.

Pneumonia, falls on the icy pavements, hypothermia, and car crashes all added to the increase in business. The deliveries became commonplace and so regular she hardly left her office to see them.

However, when all is running smoothly, and business is on the up, it's a time when Lucifer seems to delight in throwing a googly into the mix. And so it was with Joanne's business.

It was a delivery night and, on this occasion, Veronica was also in Joanne's office. They were both enjoying a drink. Out of her window Joanne watched the blacked out hearse pull up, and shortly after watched it pull away. She relaxed into her large gin and tonic, and so did Veronica as they recounted their respective days to each other.

Suddenly, blue lights lit up the whole front car park. There were two police cars but no sirens; a sure sign they wanted to catch folk red handed.

Joanne was out of her office like a shot, racing down the corridor. Veronica finished her drink and, confident Joanne was out of sight, downed Joanne's drink too before quickly following her to the foyer.

Four police officers were banging on the front and garage doors at the same time, demanding to be let in, and making enough noise to wake all the neighbours.

Flashing blue lights lit up the whole of the interior of the foyer, the car park, and the street beyond. Curtains in the normally quiet street were twitching, and front doors were being opened for the inquisitive occupants to take the evening air.

Vincent had already wheeled the delivery casket away and, when she could delay it no longer, Joanne opened the front door.

In rushed three police officers. A portlier sergeant ambled in behind them, announcing he had information that the premises was being used as a front for criminal activities.

"Such as what?" retorted Veronica, always ready for a fight with authority.

"I'm not at liberty to say, Madam."

"Miss."

"I'm sorry, but I can't say, Miss."

"Then what are you looking for?" chipped in Joanne.

"Have you just received the delivery of a coffin?"

"No!"

"But I just saw someone wheeling a coffin inside," snapped the sergeant.

"No, you didn't!" argued Joanne.

"Yes, I did," repeated the sergeant.

"What you saw was someone wheeling a casket inside. They are completely different! A casket has four sides and two ends, is oblong in shape, and constructed using better quality timber and higher standards of workmanship. A coffin has six sides, is tapered at the head and feet end, meaning it is wider at the shoulders and has two ends," explained Joanne curtly.

"Well, may I see the bloody casket?"

"No, not until you tell me what you are looking for."

A real fight was brewing. The tension in the air was painful.

At that moment Vincent wheeled the casket back into the foyer. This was the very last thing Joanne wanted to see, but it was too late. He stopped the casket immediately in front of the angry sergeant.

"Is this the coffin or casket – whatever - that was recently delivered?" the sergeant asked, putting his hand upon it.

A much calmer Vincent took over from Joanne.

"Yes, Sir. This is the casket from the cruise ship The Crimson Rose. It had been on a one month Mediterranean cruise and this poor, unfortunate, elderly lady died on its return journey. Here are the papers. I'm sure you will find them all in order for we have the contract to look after such ill-fated passengers that never complete their trips of a lifetime."

He handed the sergeant a sheaf of papers including the lady's ticket. The casket had *Property of The Crimson Rose* stamped on a brass plate on the side.

After just a cursory glance at the papers, he asked if Vincent would open the casket.

Joanne nearly exploded with anger. "No, no, no, he won't open the casket. I forbid it. It would be against all hygiene regulations, and protocol. I will speak to your superiors. How will the family feel? How would you feel if this was a relative of yours, and anyone who felt like it could violate their peace?"

"Just open the casket or I'll impound it," demanded the police sergeant.

Vincent had already started to unscrew the first screw. As he worked his way around there was a distinct atmosphere of unease descending on the group, from both parties.

Joanne was flicking uneasy glances at Veronica, who was sending them back as fast as she received them in an 'it's nothing to do with me, I work in a care home' look.

The youngest policeman asked the sergeant if it was really necessary as the name of the ship was on the outside.

"Shut up, constable. If you can't stand the heat then get out of the kitchen," snapped the sergeant. The young policeman looked distinctly unwell and started to leave the metaphorical kitchen.

Veronica, full of sympathy, shouted after him as he left, "If you're going to throw up, don't do it in our Garden of Remembrance." She paused as he started to close the door behind him. "Use your helmet!"

Once all the screws were out, Vincent slid the lid down to expose only the head and shoulders of the occupier.

Immediately, the next youngest constable went outside, leaving just one constable and the sergeant.

What Joanne and Veronica expected to see was a mummy of

a body, all bandaged up just like the last ones. What was staring back at them was a pasty faced Elsie in a faded shroud!

"There, now what?" snapped Joanne. "You happy now?"

The sergeant went a little closer. A minute later he said, "I'm sorry for the inconvenience. Our information must have been incorrect."

Veronica felt they were on a winner so added, "Well, now you're satisfied we have a lot of work to do, so if you will excuse us, we'd like to get on." She started to shepherd them out.

"Hold on a moment," said the sergeant incredulously, "she just twitched! I swear I just saw her twitch!"

Joanne went pale. Veronica took a deep breath.

"I'm bloody sure she just twitched," he repeated angrily.

Pointing at the body the sergeant looked at Vincent for an explanation, then he looked back at the body. "It was her cheek. It twitched. I'm positive it did. Did you see it, constable?" he asked, desperate for confirmation.

"Sorry, Sir, but I wasn't exactly observing the old corpse."

"Well, bloody well pay attention!"

Vincent interjected, calmly addressing the excited sergeant. "Now, I expect you have been bobbying for a lot of years, Sergeant, and know a lot about the law and criminals. Well, I've been in this trade for many years and there isn't much anyone can tell me about dead bodies. Yes, she is twitching and she is going to twitch a lot more soon! She's now been out of a refrigerator for about twelve hours. I'll explain what happens..."

Vincent paused for effect.

"When this poor unfortunate woman died, the ship's doctor would have pronounced her dead, and they would have put her into a refrigerated container to preserve her body as soon as they could. After a few hours she would have frozen solid, at which point all her muscles would have contracted. Now, as she is defrosting, the reverse is happening and you will observe all her muscles relaxing slightly."

The sergeant was listening intently. Vincent continued.

"I understand it's very unnerving when you see it for the first time, and often relatives do not believe their nearest and dearest has actually passed away. Trust me, the longer she is defrosting the more likely you are to see movement. In fact, not only will her face move slightly, and her fingers twitch occasionally, but also her buttocks will soon relax. That's when all the gases that have been festering inside her since she died will be released. She may also burp out some of the intestinal gases from her mouth, along with some white foam. If you've never smelt festering bodily gases, trust me you won't ever get the smell out of your nostrils for weeks and weeks. You will never forget the smell. Every meal you eat will taste of her bodily gases for weeks, every drink will taste of her bodily gases for weeks and every-"

"Thank you, thank you...I've heard enough," interrupted the sergeant who was turning a little pale. "Our enquiries are complete. I'm sorry to have troubled you."

The remaining two policemen turned for the door.

At that precise moment, from inside the casket, came a fart!

A real fart. Not a tiny rumble fart like a silent murmur, nor a whisper of a fart. What came out was a real ten pints of Guinness on a night out topped up by a shish kebab from a van fart.

With their hands over their noses and mouths, the two policemen jostled to get through the door. The police exit was further hastened by another fart, not so violent this time but definitely another fart.

Veronica had to bite her lip to hold back an involuntary laugh, whilst Joanne looked incomprehensibly at Vincent who was completely composed.

When the police were out of the door, Joanne and Veronica peeped into the casket.

Elsie opened her eyes and winked at them.

They watched the police cars drive off and, once they were completely clear, Vincent lifted the casket lid completely off and leaned it up against the wall. He then lifted the sides off, showing that the casket top and sides could be screwed together, but the base was separate.

Elsie jumped down from the base of the casket in her faded shroud, demonstrating how she had managed to get into the replacement casket and lower the sides with the lid already screwed down.

Vincent explained they had rehearsed the moves many times, for such an event as this, and he had to admit this had been an exemplary performance. He did a high five with Elsie and they both bowed to the applause and congratulations from Veronica and Joanne.

Further explanation revealed that this was just a replacement casket they had permanently set up for when it was needed. Elsie just attached different ships' names onto the side of the casket, slipped on a shroud and some powder, and jumped inside.

Four big gins were poured to ease the tension, and the re-run of the evening started with laughter. The four of them became louder and louder as the bottle emptied.

"Where did you learn all that stuff about coffins and caskets, Jo Jo?" asked a very impressed Veronica.

"I listened to a very good teacher, didn't I Vincent?"

Vincent smiled coyly.

"But what about that fart?" asked Veronica. "What kind of gadget makes such a realistic fart? There must be a massive gas cylinder in the coffin with you."

"Oh, sorry, that was just little old me," giggled Elsie, turning pink. "Piccalilli and salami sandwiches. My favourite."

16

Joanne struggled with the keys to a safe housed in an unused back office at the funeral parlour. It was a dingy, windowless office, with a low wattage light bulb in the centre of a peeling ceiling. She had passed the office door several times in the last few weeks but, with everything else going on, it kept flitting out of her mind.

Today, as it was quiet, she had opened the door and switched the light on. It was furnished with one chair at a small desk, under the centre light.

In the corner was a safe. A big, black, intriguing Chubb safe. A safe full of promise. A safe bulging with mystery, intrigue and wealth. Diamonds, rubies, gold, silver; her imagination was running wild, which fuelled her determination to open it.

Having tried every key possible in the building, in frustration she admitted the safe had beaten her. Not a situation with which she was familiar. In desperation, she decided she needed Vincent's help, otherwise she was likely to break a key in the lock.

"I'll try," he offered, "but only Mr Gordon opened it."

The ring of keys was turned over and over to find the elusive right one. Joanne thought there couldn't be more keys to the Bastille, which only heightened her resolve.

After an hour they both admitted the safe had defeated them.

"Will Elsie know?" asked a very cross Joanne.

"Not a clue. As I said, only Mr Gordon came in here."

"But what's in it?"

"No idea. I've hardly ever been in this office, and never when the safe was open. I'll arrange a locksmith to come and undo it in the morning if you like? However, they may have to cut a hole in the side to open it and I did hear that they set fire to everything in the safe of a friend of mine so, in the end, there was no point inviting a locksmith in the first place."

"Thank you for recounting the unsuccessful story of your friend, Vincent," said Joanne, with a touch of sarcasm.

Having only just discovered the big fridge and its hoard of ancient money, followed by the highly irregular deliveries, Joanne was in no hurry to invite a complete stranger into her business premises who might inadvertently uncover who knew what. She needed to open the safe herself for peace of mind.

Then she had an idea: Godfrey Wendover. He would know which key it was, surely. If he just identified the correct key, she could open the safe herself.

Joanne decided she would broach the idea of approaching Godfrey with Veronica.

That evening, Joanne and Veronica sat together on the sofa chatting about the day, each charged with a drink, when Joanne posed the question. The answer was not what she wanted to hear.

"No, I won't. Not a chance, and you mustn't either," snapped Veronica at Joanne.

"Why not?"

"Because his wife's on her death bed, that's why not! She's receiving end of life care at the home, that's why not! She hasn't long to live, that's why not!"

"But it'll only take him a minute. I'm sure he wouldn't mind just pointing out the right key. He could do it while he's still holding Mrs Tan's hand, or whatever her name is. He doesn't need to leave her. There are hundreds on the ring so I don't have the foggiest idea where to start. Nor does Vincent."

"No. It's not fair on either of them. Anyway, what's the hurry?"

"I've decided the parlour needs a face lift inside and out, and I don't want any slap-happy-emulsion-wally getting a lucky punt at the safe while I'm out," explained Joanne curtly. "Neither do I want him telling all his low life mates about the challenge of a big Chubb safe that can't be opened. I can imagine a bunch of wannabe safe crackers queuing up to have a pop. If one has a lucky hit and empties it before I even get a chance to see inside, I wouldn't know if anything had been stolen or not. Come on, Veronica, just for old time's sake."

"It's not right. It seems insensitive at this time."

"Come on, Veronica. You want a top up?"

Veronica relented slightly. "I'm really not happy about this. If it's not the right time, or she's too poorly, I'm not approaching him. Understand?"

"Yeah, yeah, whatever. Have it your way."

"By the way, you're right Jo Jo - this place really does need revitalising and bringing into the 20th century. It needs lightening up with some brighter electric light bulbs, and sprucing up with some gay colours and new thick carpets. Even for a funeral parlour it's a pretty gloomy and dismal place. Are you going to do it up in a happy-go-lucky ramshackle sort of way, or shall we forget the last painters you employed for cash and do it ourselves?"

"Shut up, Veronica!"

"Whilst we're talking about image, perhaps you could get Elsie into some sort of corporate uniform rather than those very fetching, white, abattoir wellies she sports, finished off by this year's ankle length rubber apron and industrial Marigold gloves, up to her elbows in last year's colour of blood. She really is too creepy for customers to inadvertently bump into on their way to the loo."

"I'll think about it."

A few days later, in Miss Tan's bedroom, Godfrey came in quietly. Miss Tan was fast asleep. It was the perfect opportunity for Veronica to broach the subject of the safe and the keys.

"Do you mind if I ask you a question, Godfrey?"

"Ask away."

"Well, you know the safe in the back office at the funeral parlour? Joanne is trying to get into it before the office gets painted. She doesn't want a posse of wannabe safe crackers-slash-painters having a pop at it. Do you know the right key for it?" With that she pulled the huge ring from her voluminous bag and handed it to him.

He immediately found the right key and passed it back to Veronica. "That's the key. It's made of brass and hardly worn for it has virtually never been used, but it won't do you any good."

"Why not?" asked a confused Veronica.

"It's the most cantankerous safe ever invented. Even with the right key you have to tilt the safe a bit to the left, and when the key has been turned a half a turn you have to lower it down and then tilt it backwards. It must have taken me about two weeks the first time. Gordon used to use it to stash papers in, I think. I haven't been in it for years and years."

"That's jiggered that plan then because Jo Jo'll never be able to open it."

A daring thought was forming in Godfrey's mind. "However, maybe I could pop over when everyone has gone home one evening, open the safe, and creep away before anyone sees me. What do you think?"

There was excitement in his voice at the thought of getting out of the care home for just a little while. Also, he was intrigued as to the safe's contents, which may be a lead into what else his brother Gordon had been up to.

"No way, you're not leaving here on my account, or Jo Jo's.

There's no way I want that to happen. Whatever would Miss Tan think if she woke and neither of us were here?"

"Tan, as you well know Veronica, has an evening nap at 7.00 pm, just before you come to work. I'll be in and out in a flash. We'll be away for no more than thirty minutes. As long as there's nobody at the funeral parlour, what could possibly go wrong?"

Veronica shook her head, "Oh, how I hate it when someone in my life says what could possibly go wrong. Anyway, what else did Gordon keep in the safe?"

"Search me. Gordon used to come over at night, and I think he used it to hide things he didn't want found in his other office if it was ever raided by the police. It could be bursting with diamonds, or cash from the deliveries, or drugs, or jewellery. Or, more likely, it's empty."

Veronica hesitantly said, "Tomorrow then, at 6.45 pm. Dress in something inconspicuous."

During the conversation Miss Tan had stirred and eventually woke. She squeezed Godfrey's hand and whispered, "You go my darling, I'll be fine. You'll have to get out from here one day. It'll be a little adventure for you."

The next evening came and, at 6.45 pm, Veronica arrived to collect Godfrey. Out he came dressed as a painter, in brand new white overalls and a navy beret.

"How long is it since you've been outside these four walls?" she asked him at the sight of his outfit.

"Not since Gordon died. When Tan found out Gordon had died, she phoned me immediately and said, 'Get home now. Gordon's dead. Nobody must see you. Come home as quickly as you can.' I was out of my office in a second and came here. It's a good job this old house is as big as it is, otherwise I would have gone nuts."

At the funeral parlour the lights were all out but the garage door had been deliberately left open by Joanne. As they drew into the garage, Joanne was standing there to meet them in the shadows.

Veronica had told Joanne of the plan, but Joanne insisted on being there to thank Godfrey in person. There was a level of curiosity too, meeting the twin of her recently departed husband for the first time ever. She opened the passenger door and went ashen.

"Gordon?" she stuttered.

"No, I'm Godfrey and I'm very pleased to meet you, Joanne. My brother Gordon said you made him very happy in the short time you two were together."

Godfrey put his hand out to shake hers. It was a good job he did for he just caught her as her eyes closed and her knees buckled. Veronica caught her other arm and between them they sat her down on a coffin in the corner of the room.

Godfrey brought her a glass of water, which he helped her to sip. When her eyes did partially open, she tried to focus on Godfrey, but passed out again.

Veronica helped Joanne move her head between her knees. Looking up at Godfrey she said, "Come to think of it you really are remarkably like Gordon, you know."

"Yes, we were always playing pranks on our parents and the teachers. We caused chaos wherever we went, and got away with murder in school. We were called 'those damned Wendover twins'."

Joanne started to come around again and this time insisted on getting up. She moved across to Godfrey and mumbled, "I'm very pleased to meet you, too."

She was trying to come to terms with the spit of her recently departed husband holding her hand. It took a few moments but she regained her composure and in true Joanne style bluntly asked, "Why the hell are you wearing white overalls and a French beret?"

"Veronica said you had decorators in so I thought I would dress appropriately."

Joanne looked at Veronica and shook her head. "Whatever. Now, can you open the safe?"

"Of course, but I don't have much time."

"Let's go then. Here are the keys."

Godfrey accepted the keys, rifled through the bunch in the dim light of the hallway, and selected the correct brass one.

They all hurried along the corridor and into the office, where the smell of fresh gloss paint and emulsion was overpowering in the poky room. White dust sheets covered everything.

Godfrey snatched the dust sheet off the safe, knelt down, put the key in the lock and then, putting all his weight against the left-hand side of the safe, spragged his feet against the wall. He then pushed with all his might. Despite his age he was still quite agile, and moved about with the suppleness of a much younger man.

The safe tilted slightly and the key moved further into the lock. The audience watched in awe. Then he put his weight against the front of the safe and tilted the safe slightly backwards. When it righted itself the door miraculously opened. Never in a million years would Joanne have found out how to open it.

"There, see, it always works," smiled Godfrey, getting off his knees.

Immediately, Joanne was pushing him out of the way and ferreting around inside the safe, scooping up armfuls of papers and laying them out on the dust sheet-covered desk under the light.

Suddenly, a pair of car headlights lit up the outer room, and four car tyres gravelled to a stop. The three looked up at the same time. Who on earth could it be at this time of night?

"You're not expecting a delivery, are you?" asked Godfrey.

"Not that I know of."

"That's Vincent's car. I'd recognise it anywhere," said Godfrey.

"There are two people in the car," said Veronica from the window, "and they're getting out. It is just Vincent and Elsie. We'd better let them in before they think we're burglars and raise an alarm with the whole neighbourhood. We don't want the local plod around here again."

Veronica let them in through the garage doors, asking what they were doing there at this time of night.

"We're here to see Godfrey," said Elsie.

Stunned silence. "How the hell did you know he was alive? And, even if you knew he was still alive, how did you know he was going to be here tonight?"

Vincent replied, "You should know that Miss Joanne's office

phone rings in the garage and, before I could put it down, I heard you and Miss Joanne talking about him coming over here tonight. And we're not stupid, are we Elsie?"

Elsie shook her head. "No, we're not, and I'm really excited to see him at last. We've gone along with the Gordon and Godfrey thing for years and we were really sorry when he had to disappear, but we understood. Godfrey might have been a bit of a shambles as a businessman, but we loved working with him and were so sorry when it all had to end."

By this time they had all walked to the back office. Vincent walked purposefully over to Godfrey and shook his hand, saying he was really pleased to see he was OK but they were both sorry to hear about Miss Tan.

Elsie rushed over to Godfrey and hugged him for a long time. Tears were in her eyes and she wouldn't let him go. She couldn't speak but kept looking up and touching his face affectionately, to check it was really him.

"What?" asked Joanne. "You've both known about the Gordon and Godfrey switch for a long time?"

"Of course. Since day one. But it was none of our business so we just went along with the charade."

Vincent, Elsie and Godfrey chatted like old friends about days gone past. He was particularly amused about the police raid and the way the funeral parlour was now being run. Soon it was time for them to leave.

"If you can, please come and see us again," pleaded Elsie. Then the pair waved back to Godfrey as they drove off.

Oblivious to what was happening between Godfrey, Vincent and Elsie, Joanne had emptied the top shelves of the safe of all their contents. Yet, try as she might in the dimly lit room, she was unable to read a word of the faded documents.

"Let's go along to my office and see what Gordon was up to," she announced insensitively. "Veronica, you bring that big box that's in the bottom of the safe."

"You'll be OK with all those heavy papers, will you, Jo Jo?" snapped Veronica sarcastically.

Joanne and Godfrey marched briskly to Joanne's office where they spread the papers out on the acre of desk. The bright green desk light lit up the copperplate writing of the first manuscript:

Enacted this day the twelfth of April 1965.
By Government and by the power invested in me are enclosed the deeds and codicils for the purchase of number 45, Promenade Walk, in the County of West Sussex, England.

"It's a set of deeds for the purchase of one of those big, old, rundown houses on the prom. They're massive but most are derelict, or limping along just surviving as down-market hostels. They're a real eyesore. Actually, it looks as if there are five sets of deeds, one for each of the houses," said Joanne.

Her accountant's brain was in overdrive. Anything not identified in Gordon's will should surely go to her - her solicitor had said as much when she was trying to deal with Gordon's grasping ex-wife. "If it is not declared in Gordon's will, then the family will have no claim on it after a number of years," he had said.

They had done very nicely from his estate, and tied as much

as they knew about back into the family before she and Gordon were married.

So, she mused thoughtfully, I am now the proud owner of five properties on the promenade then?

Veronica reversed through the door and into the office. Struggling with the heavy box, she banged it down on the side table and promptly sat down, exhausted. The box measured two feet long and a foot square.

"What have I missed?"

"Oh, nothing. What's in the box then?" avaricious Joanne asked.

"I've been carrying it, not examining it," Veronica snapped.

Ignoring the comment, Joanne cleared the desk of the papers and nodded to Veronica to bring the box to the desk.

Godfrey felt the temperature in the room suddenly rise between the two of them, and took it upon himself to lift the heavy box onto the desk.

Lightening the abrupt change of mood, he said, "There, now let's see if it's full of diamonds or Gordon's unfinished lunch."

There was no key and the lid opened easily. No wonder the box was so heavy; the lid was lined with lead, as were the sides and ends. Godfrey lowered the lid carefully down onto the desk. Inside, something was wrapped in sheepskin.

Godfrey lifted the parcel out and set it gently on the desk. He then proceeded to unwrap the parcel by turning the contents over and over. He could see Joanne was all for tearing the wrapping off like a petulant child at Christmas, but he continued cautiously. He was thinking that if his brother had seen fit to hide the box in the safe, then its contents will most definitely have value.

There seemed to be two identical items inside, wrapped separately in yellowing, soft sheepskin. He finished unwrapping the first object and carefully set it down on the desk. It was gold coloured and dome shaped, and all around the object small bells hung from tiny cantilevers. When upright it stood about fifteen inches tall.

The other package was the same. Standing side by side in the light from the desk lamp, the two artefacts exuded a religious aura. They were very well crafted and demanded a timeless reverence. A musty, church odour came from the sheepskins; the smell of absorbed incense, vellum, and aged books all rolled into one.

The smell brought back memories for Godfrey, from when he and his brother had been dragged, protesting, to church every Sunday morning by their parents, whatever the weather.

The two of them would mumble their way through the hymns, and turn the endless pages of the order of service, desperate to escape the torture and get outside.

The distant memory conjured up the smell of elderly parishioners dressed in their rarely worn best coats. Coats guarded from the voracious appetites of winged insects by the toxic vapour of naphthalene, moth balls.

Positioned directly in front of the boys had been aged, carpeted kneelers, each embroidered with a religious message, and each wheezing its individual odour when squashed. Along with the well-thumbed hymn books, and order of service books, the timbale of odours combined to exude a sacred smell.

The artefacts in front of him presented that same timeless, ecclesiastical smell too.

"What are they?" asked Joanne, peering closely.

"Well," said Godfrey, "I think they're Torah Finial Bells, but I can't be sure. I believe they're Jewish and were used in conjunction with prayer scrolls. Another name for them I think is Torah Rimonim, but my memory's not that good."

Veronica tweaked one of the tiny bells and said, "I just love the dinky little bells. Oh, and look, how lovely, the sides are decorated with little footballs. That's sweet."

"No, they aren't footballs," Godfrey replied patiently, "they're pomegranates. That's why I'm pretty sure these are Jewish. The pomegranate is the Jewish symbol of fruitfulness."

"How do you know all this?" asked Veronica, entranced that any one person in the world would have such knowledge, and even more impressed by his powers of recall. She had difficulty remembering a shopping list, let alone two different names of a Jewish religious symbol.

"Oh, I've never seen one before, not even a picture, but one of the soldiers I escaped with was Jewish and he told me about enemy soldiers raiding Jewish homes and taking paintings, silverware and jewels."

"Really?" Asked Veronica.

"Yes, they also went into synagogues and stole the religious relics. Ephraim was his name. He was so angry that any country in the world could do such a thing to his religion. The four of us had so much time to kill because we only travelled at night. Ephraim spent some of the time describing the Jewish religion, and family life as a Jew. It was fascinating. I think talking helped him to believe he was going to get home one day. Ephraim also talked about some of the religious ornaments and their symbolism. I clearly remember him, with tears running down his cheeks, recalling when the soldiers stole the Torah Finial Bells from his local synagogue. He remembered his gentle mother pleading with the soldiers not to take them, but she was pushed out of the way like a dog. The enemy soldiers stashed their loot in caves and cellars and then bricked them up."

"How do you think Gordon got hold of them then?" asked Joanne.

"That's a much more difficult puzzle to untangle. We'll never know. However, what I do know is that when the soldiers were retreating in a hurry, they couldn't take the stolen items with them, so they just left everything. The less scrupulous locals knew where the stashes of paintings and gold stolen from the Jews and Gypsies were hidden so, as soon as it was safe, they broke into the caves and old cellars and helped themselves. Some of the priceless artefacts were sold on to the tommies. Most had no idea of the true value, neither buyers nor sellers."

"What happened to them?" asked Veronica.

"Some of the items were confiscated from the British soldiers by the Army and eventually returned to their rightful owners, but it was wartime and records were full of holes. It would not surprise me if some less than honourable Quartermasters sold the confiscated items on again. Some of the items were small enough to secrete inside a uniform and ended up on the black antiques market back in Blighty," explained Godfrey.

"Knowing Gordon though, I don't think he'd have been interested in the odd item, he'd have wanted to know where the whole stash was and, once he'd found it, he would be keen to set up a means of getting it all shipped to England. This could be the first and only item from the enemy's stash, or it could be the last item. We'll never know. He always was on the lookout for a deal."

"We must try and find their rightful owner and return them," suggested Veronica.

"You can dream on!" snapped an indignant Joanne. "They belonged to Gordon. He could have bought them. They could have been a present to him. He might have been hiding them for someone else. There are a dozen different reasons why he had them. We don't want to be too hasty."

Realising the two of them were less than impressed by her arguments, and were watching her incredulously, she suggested they put them back and consider their future at a later date.

"Hey, I've just seen the time. I need to get back to Tan," said Godfrey.

17

"Your Gordon is turning out to have been a bit of a lad by all accounts," Veronica exclaimed, as she drove quickly back along the winding country roads, trying to take Gordon's mind off the elapsed time.

"Yes, in many respects we were chalk and cheese, and if we weren't identical twins it would lead you to wonder."

They both laughed.

More small talk instigated by Veronica made the journey pass quickly. Godfrey found Veronica easy to chat to as they drove along. She was honest and said things as they came into her head.

They had spent many hours together alongside Tan as she slept in her morphine-induced dream world, but when she was awake the three of them enjoyed each other's company.

Veronica's lively demeanour and brightness was a tonic to Tan. She had no airs or graces and treated all folk alike. Whenever Veronica came into the bedroom, she was always cheerful. They liked that. Veronica had been a real diamond to Tan and nothing was genuinely too much trouble, whereas Joanne, Godfrey decided, was a much more difficult woman to fathom.

Before Gordon married Joanne, he confided in Godfrey that Joanne could be a really caring person, but when money was at stake she was single minded. She became absolutely focussed to the point of being obsessive.

Although Godfrey had only just met Joanne, he believed he had just experienced that financial focus when he started to open the safe. She was all but salivating at the thought of possible riches and wealth, and craning her whole body to see inside before the thick, steel door was fully opened. Her eyes had become narrowed, dilated, fixed.

Veronica and Godfrey wound their way through the tree-lined lanes towards the Bethesda Care Home. As they drove though the aged, stone, gate pillars at the lodge, pulsating blue lights from two ambulances lit up the private entrance at the side.

Godfrey was immediately straining in his seat belt. The blue lights flashed around and around, reflecting on every window in the front of the building. The silent blue lights showed ghostly patients watching the gloomy spectacle from various windows, some standing, some sitting, all wondering if their turn to leave this earthly departure lounge was far away.

"Oh, please God, no," wailed Godfrey. "I should never have left her. I'll never forgive myself. She won't go to hospital, she said so. Tan made me promise never to let anyone take her to hospital to die. I won't let her go."

Veronica's car crunched to a standstill near the private entrance, but before it had completely stopped Godfrey was out of the car and running towards the ambulance. The paramedics were sliding a completely covered body on a stretcher into the ambulance, and one of the paramedics stopped Godfrey from getting any closer.

"No, no, no, no," Godfrey wept.

With his hand firmly on Godfrey's shoulder the paramedic said, "Sorry, Sir, but when we found her she was on the floor by the bed. She must have tumbled out and hit her head on the side table. We did arrive in time, but by then she was very weak and her heart must have just given up. We tried for a long while to bring her back, but had to pronounce her dead about thirty minutes ago. I'm very sorry for your loss, but we really did everything we could."

"It's my fault, it's all my fault," he groaned. "I should never have gone out, I should never have left her." Godfrey sobbed and dropped to his knees with his head in his hands, unable to bear the burden of grief and guilt.

By this time Veronica was by his side at the back of the ambulance. She knew there was absolutely nothing she could do, nothing she could say, except to just be there for him.

Godfrey was distraught; his whole body was shaking from his sobs. He had lost his soul mate and worse - he hadn't been there with her at the end. He imagined her lying there calling for him, and another surge of guilt wracked his body.

Veronica crouched beside him and just kept a hand on his shoulder - a contact to tell him she was there.

One of the paramedics then gestured for Veronica to talk to

him away from Godfrey. He asked if the lady was a relative of hers. When she said no, he then asked if Veronica worked at the care home. She replied that she had worked there for some time, and was the night assistant.

He then asked why the lady had been left alone in such a state. He went on to ask if the care home had a protocol for elderly patients who were on regular morphine medication. He wasn't letting go and went on to ask what time span of discretion was applied for checks on elderly patients at the care home. More questions followed. Why were no staff with her? Didn't the lady have a history that dictated a comprehensive care plan?

Veronica had also lost someone who was very close to her and she was in a vulnerable place as well as Godfrey. She stood there, not knowing how to reply to any of the paramedic's questions, and feeling responsible for everything. She was close to tears.

Oh, how Veronica wished she had been wearing normal clothes and not her work uniform, so that someone else could bear the brunt of the justifiable verbal onslaught from this paramedic. But he was right. They were wrong. They should never have left her. This should have been a normal evening and right now, if she hadn't asked Godfrey to leave Miss Tan, they would all be chatting and laughing together in her bedroom.

She should have told Joanne a flat no! She felt so responsible, she felt accountable, and she felt liable. No, she felt unreliable; she had let Miss Tan down.

She wanted to cry, but not there, not now. She would cry alone, at home, when the reality of what had happened sunk in. She would cry alone, not only for the loss of someone she had come to care for deeply, but because she hadn't been with Miss Tan at the end.

Out of the corner of her eye she saw the care home manager walking towards the ambulance carrying some papers. This would allow her to escape from the interrogation.

The manager called Veronica over. "Sad way to go, eh?" she said.

Noticing Veronica was close to tears she rubbed her arm sympathetically. "It doesn't get any easier does it? No matter how many times you see it. I don't know how many times I must have told her that after her medicine she was to stay still and not move. This isn't the first time you know. She's done it before, trying to get out of bed afterwards, not knowing what she was doing or where she was. Morphine's a strange medication and affects folk in different ways on different days. Some days it's off to sleep in an instant, and others it's as though the patient has a new lease of life and believe they can do almost anything. They believe themselves to be invincible."

Veronica had stopped listening to the care home manager prattling on trying to be sympathetic in her own way, but her upset mind chose to re-run one of the last sentences. "Get out of bed? What do you mean get out of bed? Miss Tan never got out of bed!"

"Miss Tan?" said the care home manager, frowning. "It's not Miss Tan."

"Who the hell's on the stretcher then?"

"It's Miss Violet Ann. Oh, you...you thought it was Miss Tan? Oh no. She's fine. Very upset about the loss of her sister, but OK. I checked on her myself just before you got here. One of the other nurses is staying with her now."

Veronica felt sick. Sick with relief. Sick with shock. Sick with guilt that she felt relieved it was someone, anyone else. Veronica went over to Godfrey at the ambulance and took his arm. "Come away, Godfrey."

"No, I won't leave her. It's all my fault. I should never have left her. I didn't say goodbye."

"Godfrey, come away with me now. It's not Tan, it's Violet Ann."

* * *

Not long after, things changed.

The funeral parlour business had created a momentum of its own. The customer service was being delivered at a new level, the costs were competitive, and Joanne's business acumen had driven the business to new heights.

She had spent some money on the décor of the parlour, and the investment was paying her back handsomely. The rooms were light and airy and fittingly decorated, and appropriate, gentle music drifted through the corridors and chapel of rest.

Joanne had also set aside a little place for clients who broke down and wished to be alone. This tasteful room was complimented with soft, neutral coloured furnishings and boxes of tissues.

The Club had been given a long overdue makeover and the money was now tumbling in, being carefully recorded and banked with the full name and address of each member.

Elsie flatly refused to don corporate wear, but conceded to

use the back stairs and corridors when moving about the parlour.

Astonishingly, Elsie was occasionally mentioned in dispatches for the quality of her sandwiches at the wakes. That's because now there were no 'volley vont dooferies', or potatoes wrapped in tin foil with cheese and pineapple chunks impaled on cocktail sticks. Pickled onions and crisps were also an absolute no-no.

The sandwiches were now filled with recognisable fillings, cut diagonally, and presented beautifully with some garnish. The wake tables always looked professional.

The wine had been ratcheted up in quality from Liebfraumilch to Sancerre, and the red upgraded from cheap Vin Rouge to Malbec and, what's more, all the clients were happy to pay the extra for a quality send off.

Behind the scenes there was order, and proper processes. Now there were Contracts of Employment, Employment Policies, a Conflict of Interest Policy, a Fire and Evacuation Policy, a Health and Safety Policy, and a complete set of financial accounting systems.

Joanne was happy. She was surrounded by order. She was in heaven. She was also really happy that the deliveries were coming more regularly, and that Veronica's father was slowly but surely disposing of the old coins from the big fridge. She had no idea how lucrative a numismatist's hobby could be.

Her solicitor was investigating the provenance of the five hotels on the promenade, and the only things burning a hole in the back of her mind were the Torah Finial Bells.

Her business had become busier and busier to the point

that Joanne was beginning to consider employing a manager.

All in all, Joanne's funeral parlour had become the funeral parlour of first choice for miles around.

All was right with the world for Joanne and, after the Miss Tan scare, it was all right with Veronica too.

18

Veronica's dad, George Puxworthy, was a down to earth, grounded man of large stature, who book-ended with his comfortably proportioned wife. Despite his powerful frame he spoke softly, not needing to impress, and he worked on the docks.

His misty, grey eyes were a legacy of working in the holds of ships levelling their cargoes of coal. When the coal trimmers used their handkerchiefs several days after the last shift worked, they were presented with a black reminder of their dusty world below decks.

Every day, George returned home with the finest eyeliner that would challenge the skills of the very best make-up artist. When down in a ship's hold with his mates, George was exactly where he wanted to be.

It was to George Puxworthy they came when a ship was listing in the dock having been overloaded on the port or starboard side.

George had a way of making the irresponsible crane driver not feel he was a complete idiot for getting the ship in such a mess, and George and his team always levelled the ship.

He wasn't the archetypal docker who downed nine pints on a Saturday night at the dock worker's institute. He didn't play dominoes at the local pub before Sunday lunch, and George rarely drank.

He worked whenever he could but he preferred to spend what other time he had with his family. He and his wife had been blessed with two daughters, as different as any two daughters could ever be.

The youngest, Molly, was studious and prim, shadowing her grandfather's slight frame and sharp brain on her father's side. Their other daughter, Veronica, was full of fun and mischief following her father's mould. Sadly, Veronica mirrored her mother's and gran's frames, both of whom were built to ride sofas.

However, they were all happy in their own way. The snug little family lived in a tiny, rented, docker's house with gran the in-law, or 'gran the out-law', as George preferred to call her.

At weekends, George sometimes worked for a demolition company driving a digger. It was here, searching amongst the rubble of an old house, he came across a Crawford's cream cracker biscuit tin full of old British coins that the original owner must have hidden many years before.

Many times he tried to locate the previous owners of the property, but they had been dead and gone for a very long time and there was no word of any relatives.

That Crawford's cream cracker tin was the find that started his interest as a numismatist. At first he thought it was a child's collection but, as he researched the coins at the library, he discovered the tin contained a Mary Queen of Scots 1567 crown valued at approximately £500. There was also a George 1st 1720 quarter guinea valued at approximately £175, a Victorian 1899 double florin valued at approximately £70, and several Victorian 1837-1901 quarter farthings valued at approximately £50 each.

He struggled to understand how something as simple as an old coin could be worth seventeen times what he earned in a long week in a ship's hold.

George's interest in the history behind the coins had been ignited. Over the next few years he spent hours in the library researching the history and value of coins. He bought and sold coins from all over the country, adding to his own collection and generating a handsome profit from all his transactions.

However, he continued to work as a coal trimmer doing the job he loved which, bearing in mind his take home pay totalled £29 after his rent had been deducted, was amazing. George was a secretive man who kept himself to himself, especially when it came to his hobby.

Over time, he had become an expert in Victorian coins and could tell a fake a mile off. He couldn't believe his good fortune when Veronica invited him to sell a mixture of coins for Joanne.

Veronica confided in him that there were many more, mainly Victorian coins, but amongst them was the odd William IV and George IV penny and three-halfpenny pieces. George III cartwheel two-penny pieces, valued in fine condition at approximately £150 each, were his favourite.

He liked to turn them over and over again in his gnarled fingers wondering how many hands the chunky coins had passed through during their lifetime. One two-penny coin filled his palm; they weren't called cartwheel tuppences for nothing. He pondered how many goods had been paid for with such a coin. He wondered how many day's labour it would have bought during its early lifetime. He mused how many wedding rings had been paid for with the hefty coin being part of the deal.

Throughout the 1960s and 1970s there had been an upsurge in the interest in coins. This had been prompted by the lead up to decimalisation of British coinage in 1971, everyone believing the old coins would one day be worth something.

So far, he had sold about £5,000 worth of coins for Joanne, and insisted on not flooding the market place for his personal contacts would soon become suspicious. Just like his nature he took a pedestrian approach to disposing of the coins.

Veronica understood completely. Joanne did not!

19

Surprisingly, the sudden death of Miss Violet Ann affected everyone at Bethesda far more than anyone expected for weeks. It was the sole topic of conversation amongst the residents. At each mealtime, comments were whispered across the dining tables with the occasional furtive glance heavenwards.

"I didn't think she was that ill. She did like a tipple though. Perhaps she died of a G and T overdose? Anyway, she never had a kind word to say to anyone. They say she was dreadful to the staff, absolutely dreadful."

"You shouldn't speak ill of the dead because you may be joining her sooner than you think! She's probably listening to you this very minute."

"Perhaps you're right. I suppose she wasn't all bad."

"The ambulance was here as fast as a fire engine. They tell me the paramedics worked on her for a full hour!"

When the coroner's court eventually announced accidental death, the findings were a huge relief to all the staff and the care home manager. Once again, their world buzzed with normal life.

As neither Miss Tan nor Godfrey could attend Miss Violet Ann's funeral, Veronica reluctantly offered to go in their places. She didn't relish the thought, but to make them happy she said she would attend and report straight back.

Back at her flat, Veronica's wardrobe was populated by slimming, dark clothes, so choosing something suitably black for the event was easy. She was representing Miss Tan and Godfrey so took extra special care with her appearance, and even decided an annual polish of her black patent shoes was appropriate.

Uncharacteristically, she left plenty of time to walk to the church promising herself that, despite the occasion, she would enjoy the stroll.

The village church was a pretty church, the best of everything rural England had to offer.

Neat rows of tended graves, inside a low walled cemetery, faced the church, not all leaning against perimeter walls for ease of mowing, but upright and square in their original places. Marble, granite or simple wooden crosses - it didn't matter how plain or ornate - were all tended with the same level of care.

In front of every headstone was positioned a small vase for wild flowers which, Veronica had been told by Miss Tan, was filled every year when the occupant's birthday came around. The vases were lovingly arranged by the wonderful, old, much loved ex-vicar of the parish.

Knowing the difficulty and expense of obtaining a gardener,

he had volunteered his services to look after the cemetery when he retired.

The task had given him a new lease of life. He spent his mornings working there and his afternoons walking the parish lanes collecting wild flowers. The lychgate was newly varnished and exuded care, love and the memories of happy occasions.

Veronica only wished every church in England could be as well looked after, and wondered about the kindly, retired vicar who put wild flowers on the graves of those who everyone else had forgotten.

At Christmas and Easter time the little church held about seventy worshippers at a squash, so as Veronica approached she wondered if she was a little late and all the mourners were already inside.

She pushed open the protesting, iron clad, wooden church door to reveal, through the dark interior, that the congregation was a meagre number of mourners. So meagre, in fact, they didn't even fill the front row on one side.

Shortly after Veronica had settled into the front pew next to another care home worker, Miss Violet Ann's casket was wheeled in by Vincent and his sombre team to unidentifiable organ chords.

Once in position in front of the altar, Vincent's team bowed reverently, turned as one, and departed. Veronica wished they would stay just to make up the numbers.

The service was a solemn affair in the seemingly cavernous, empty space. Unfamiliar hymns were inaudibly mumbled into hymnbooks, with the vicar single-handedly trying to make up for the lack of a choir, congregation and consequential poor volume.

His eulogy was disjointed, as it always is when the vicar hasn't the foggiest idea who the unfortunate departed was. Nor had he completed sufficient research to make it even vaguely interesting. It was a sort of horoscope eulogy; one that fits all.

Every time the vicar needed to use Violet Ann's name whilst extolling her imagined virtues, he paused and carefully checked her name in his notes. The pause only exaggerated his lack of rehearsal; surely evidence of a previous, career-limiting, funeral calamity where he probably used the wrong name over and over again, thought Veronica.

How does the weather know the exact second a funeral service is over, Veronica wondered? In contrast with the wonderful, bright summer's day as she walked to the service, a downpour started at precisely the moment the casket was being wheeled out of the church into the graveyard.

Veronica wondered whether it was retribution for Violet Ann or retribution for the mourners. Perhaps it was Violet Ann's last tantrum?

Veronica had, over the last few weeks, spent more time than expected with the truculent woman, as finding staff to cope with her outbursts had been almost impossible for the care home manager.

Veronica's approach was to be completely oblivious to her outbursts. An approach which, over time, morphed into her feeling sorry for the quarrelsome woman. The tantrums were solely attention seeking, so when Veronica ignored them they soon lost their impact. It allowed her to see the real Violet Ann; a frightened lady who was spending her last days alone.

Veronica thought she and Violet Ann had eventually come to a mutual understanding and there were times she even enjoyed her company, believing the fondness was marginally reciprocated. Veronica remembered bravely telling her that she had a lovely smile and she should smile more often.

In totally unsuitable heels, Veronica slipped and stumbled along the grassy path on her way to the graveside as she tried to keep up with the goat-footed, gabardine-coated, dry, casket bearers.

At the graveside, she shuffled around the gaping mouth of the grave along with other mourners, manoeuvring to be alongside someone with an umbrella and praying she didn't slip and fall.

Time at the wet graveside ticked past slowly for all the mourners, especially Veronica who shared the tiny umbrella of the shortest care home assistant ever.

With knees bent slightly to level the difference in height, Veronica needed to keep tilting the umbrella handle slightly to avoid the rivulets of rain icing their way down her inappropriate, black, silk, summer blouse. Through gritted teeth, the rightful owner of the umbrella insisted upon returning it to its original position, and the friendly tussle continued for the duration of the interment.

Under a dark, wet sky, one solitary wreath brightened the scene but not the mood. Veronica believed if Miss Tan had been there, she would have been happy with her sister's flower arrangement but sad it was the only tribute.

After the service the wake, such as it was, organised by Joanne and Elsie, was held in the village hall and fed just five people; three from the care home, the vicar and Veronica, rather than the thirty mourners anticipated.

Veronica sidled over to Joanne and furtively asked if she could eat the sandwiches. A non-committal shake of the head was her reply but Veronica noticed that Joanne wasn't eating anything.

It wasn't a yes or a no so Veronica tucked in. A free buffet was always seen as a challenge but even her voracious appetite made only a small dent in the spread on the groaning table. Nevertheless, she made a more valiant effort with the wine, despatching herself with alacrity.

After the wake and inconsequential small talk, it was Elsie who announced that the mourners were welcome to take some of the food home if they wanted to.

As if by magic one large, well-worn, supermarket carrier bag, and an equally large freezer bag, were produced from under the vicar's flowing cassock and he proceeded to professionally clear the table saying, "Every morsel helps to stretch a vicar's meagre stipend."

Joanne and Veronica watched in amazement as the table was hoovered clean. What little food did remain was carefully bagged up and taken back to the care home by the assistants.

As promised, Veronica reported back that evening to Miss Tan and Godfrey, avoiding eye contact with either. She enthusiastically told them that the church had been well supported by about eight rows of friends, family and locals. Miss Tan's beautiful flower arrangement had stolen the show of all the other wreaths and bouquets, and had been left in a prominent position at her sister's graveside.

She went on to say that the whole church had been decked out with bright flowers and smelled of summer. Veronica said the vicar had been amazing and spoke with true warmth as though he had known Miss Violet Ann all his life.

She also reported that the singing was so good that if you shut your eyes you could be forgiven for thinking you were listening to the choir of Westminster Cathedral.

Veronica's fingers ached from being crossed behind her back, but she continued saying that during the whole of the interment the sun shone brightly to say goodbye to Miss Violet Ann, only starting to drizzle a little when the graveside service was completely over.

Miss Tan smiled at her exaggerations and embellishments and squeezed Veronica's hand after noticing her tell-tale muddy shoes and rat-tailed hair.

20

Two days later, Miss Tan tentatively asked if Veronica would be so kind as to represent her at the reading of her sister's will.

Veronica at first declined as she had never attended the reading of any will, and knew nothing of the protocol or dress code, but after some coaching from Miss Tan she reluctantly agreed to attend the formality. Light-heartedly, she suggested she would soon be asking the care home manager for a clothing allowance for all the official engagements she was now attending.

The will was to be read at the Mainwaring family solicitor's office in the high street, which Veronica would be able to walk to from her flat.

The day of the reading was bright and sunny and as she walked she swung her cavernous bag containing peppermints, liquorice all sorts, coconut mushrooms and a pen and pad.

Inside the solicitor's office, she was escorted by a receptionist up to the partner's boardroom. Their conversation was chatty as they walked along the corridors, and Veronica was surprised to hear that everyone else had arrived much earlier and some were even on their second cup of tea.

The receptionist complained she had replenished the biscuit plate several times already. Apparently, they were all seated in silence. The receptionist whispered to Veronica that she wasn't late; the others had all arrived far too early.

Veronica was expecting similar numbers to the funeral, but reminded herself that when money was being distributed at the reading of any will, long lost relatives would crawl from afar to be there. Then she admonished herself for thinking like that, for not all families were like her gran's side of the family.

As the two of them arrived at the door of the boardroom, Veronica wondered what reception she would meet on the other side.

On entering, she saw eighteen stony-faced people already seated in the room. The taciturn attendees' eyes followed her every move.

She walked slowly around the expansive walnut table and found the only empty chair. Having been furnished with a cup of tea, she sat down.

Eighteen pairs of questioning eyes were silently asking the same questions: Who was she? What was a stranger doing here? What right had she to be here? Was she a distant relation?

Following a swift scan of the people, Veronica determined there wasn't a soul she recognised, but chided herself. Why would she? None of these people had been to the care home whilst she had been there.

Shortly after Veronica had settled and began drinking her tea with as little noise as possible, a very tall, balding man dressed in the broad striped uniform of a solicitor, complete with an off-white shirt with curled collar ends, and an off-centre, nondescript tie which had been tied without any knowledge of a Windsor knot, entered the room.

The solicitor started his monologue. As soon as he spoke it was obvious he had a speech impediment and pronounced every fourth word very loudly. It reminded Veronica of the Queen's Christmas Day speech.

"I had been ADVISED by my client MISS Violet Ann Mainwaring, BEFORE her unfortunate death, TO invite you all HERE today for the READING of Miss Violet ANN Mainwaring's last will AND testament, where I AM to inform you THAT you will all HEAR something to your ADVANTAGE. Thank you all FOR coming. Please will YOU all introduce yourselves AND your connection with THE deceased."

The connections, however tenuous, were embellished by the attendees and Veronica introduced herself as a Bethesda Care Home nurse representing Miss Charlotte Ann Wendover.

The introductions were, on the whole, ignored and there was shuffling and excitement in the air, for greed has a smell and an intensity all its own. Veronica had been around Joanne for long enough to recognise the signs.

An avaricious odour penetrated the room, closing in on the gathering. There was a hum of expectancy; that hum of something for nothing. All the attendees were silently waiting for the moment when piles of money would be shuffled across to each of the avid mourners by means of the croupier's tee. At this casino table of death the tee was wielded by the solicitor of the deceased.

In the minds of the attendees, plans had already been drawn up for the disposal of their windfall. Mortgages could be paid off, brand new cars could be on their drives by the weekend, cruises could be booked, holidays planned, and they would never work again.

Everyone has a dream and that day, in the solicitor's office, that dream was coming closer, for the spoils could be enormous from the disposal of half a prestigious country house with all its antique furniture. The room was politely quiet, everyone inwardly willing the solicitor to get to the juicy bit.

To pass the time attendees eyed each other furtively. Questioning thoughts about the justification for presence in the room were nearly audible. Who was going to get what? Would the shares be equal or would there be inequalities, and why would that be? What right do all these other people have being here? I'm family so will I have the greatest share?

God, this is going to be a long afternoon, Veronica groaned inwardly, popping in a peppermint before the previous coconut mushroom was entirely finished.

To pass the time, she started to count the solicitor's droning words. One, two three four. One two three four, she mimicked in her mind. The solicitor could equally have been at home in a pulpit, she thought, and rated the funeral vicar of a few days ago against this solicitor in their ability to bore. She decided they were on par.

Were they born boring or did they go to special training schools? She wondered if they had to pass an ecumenical or legal module on being dull. Maybe they needed a Masters. Perhaps they were injected with some tincture prior to their convocation ceremony, or was being boring just hereditary?

On and on droned the solicitor with the will's introduction as Veronica continued zoning out, moving on to wonder about the lovely, old vicar and the flowers arranged on the birthday graves. Until she heard her own name.

"And to Miss Veronica Sidero Puxworthy, I leave my half of the Bethesda Care Home."

There was consternation in the room. Cups and saucers bounced off the table as attendees banged their fists down in temper.

The group, as one, levitated from their seats shouting, "We'll sue. It's disgraceful. It's down-right daylight robbery. Fancy taking advantage of an old lady during her last breaths."

All the fingers and scathing comments were being directed at Veronica, but the noise and anger went way over her head. She was in a surreal place, not understanding, not believing. She wasn't there; she was in the audience of a movie, she was just an onlooker, a bystander.

"They can't mean me. I'm just here to listen. Nothing to do with me," she whispered to herself.

Apparently, the eighteen distant friends and relatives, who incidentally had never visited Miss Violet Ann once in the care home, were all on a list to be invited, in person, in the event of her death.

Her solicitor had been instructed to confirm to each of them that they would learn something to their advantage, further heightening their anticipation.

This theatre had been organised for them all to watch their dreams disappear, and their imagined fortunes evaporate, whilst their inheritance was bequeathed to a complete stranger. Even the solicitor had to admit Miss Violet Ann certainly was a bizarre client.

Slowly, the solicitor regained order. Once everyone was settled, he continued saying that the only other item in Miss Violet Ann's will was her jewellery.

There was a pause, for he knew another outburst was imminent. He took a deep breath before he said, "All Miss Violet Ann's jewellery is to go to her sister, Mrs Charlotte Ann Wendover."

More consternation. This time the solicitor really struggled to be heard. Finally, his ploy was to proceed to read from a letter addressed to the rapacious audience, saying that Miss Violet Ann Mainwaring wanted them all to learn something to their advantage.

Eventually there was silence in the room for maybe, just maybe, they were wondering if there might be something else. The solicitor began to read.

"My letter is addressed to you all,

I wanted to point out that none of you have visited me in all the years I have been in the Bethesda Care Home. However, you are all here today. This indicates that my soul and company are more valuable to you in death than in life."

There was a guilty silence in the room. He continued.

"I wanted you all to hear something to your advantage."

He paused, for the pure drama of the moment, knowing what was coming next.

"It is that you should seriously consider, in your last few years, doing some good every day by keeping in touch with your friends and family. This will ensure that in your last years, and months, and weeks, and days, and hours, and minutes you will not be as lonely or as badly let down as I have been let down by you."

He concluded the letter with eulogy finality.

"Regards, Violet Ann Mainwaring, Miss."

Shuffling in the room pre-empted a soundless, guilty exit.

Finally, Veronica and the solicitor were alone. Veronica needed a drink. Did she need a drink? She turned to him.

"But why?"

The solicitor, now without a big audience, lost his nervousness and spoke normally. He said he had been summoned to the Bethesda Care Home recently and told to bring a solicitor from another practice, as a witness, to meet with the two owner sisters.

During the meeting, Miss Violet Ann's will was completely changed in Veronica's favour. Miss Tan was present the whole time and in full agreement with the changes. He explained there were three reasons that had prompted the change.

"The first reason was that if Miss Violet Ann had bequeathed her half of the Bethesda Care Home to her so-called friends and family, she was certain they would put pressure on Miss Tan to sell. Miss Tan didn't need that pressure at this stage in her life. In the case of the second reason, she also felt that if you, Veronica, owned half of the Bethesda Care Home, you would make sure that Miss Tan would be well looked after for the remainder of her days. Many times she had heard her sister laughing and couldn't fathom how anyone with such terrible leg pain could even smile, let alone laugh. But you did make her sister laugh and for that she would be forever grateful."

The solicitor recalled the third reason was early on in her employment when Veronica was told by the care home manager to take Miss Violet Ann out in her wheelchair to the promenade. Veronica winced inwardly as she remembered the incident. Again, it had not been one her finest moments but it had turned out OK.

"You and Miss Violet Ann had an altercation. She demanded to be taken to the garden, not the promenade. Apparently, you said, 'No, you and I are going to the promenade. I am the engine of this vehicle, and also the driver, and you will do as you are told for once, so sit tight and enjoy the ride'. Miss Violet Ann had not been spoken to like that for years. You also bought her an ice cream that she insisted she didn't want, but apparently started to thoroughly enjoy. Things changed suddenly when a seagull flew down and snatched it out of her hands. You burst out laughing and then another seagull swooped down and took yours."

Veronica smiled at the memory. Miss Violet Ann had been so cross when the incident occurred, and looked like thunder when she was being laughed at. But when the second seagull swooped, Miss Violet Ann also burst out laughing. The two enjoyed the rest of the day, ending up in a teashop for afternoon tea.

"So, those were the three reasons that changed her mind."

Veronica took a long, slow thoughtful walk back to her flat; she didn't want to arrive before her mind was straight. She walked to the end of the promenade and smiled to herself when she arrived at the place of the ice cream and seagull saga.

Sitting on a bench looking out to sea, she tried to fathom how on earth she had come from being a little girl in a rented house up north, where they were taught to be quiet when the rent man came knocking on a Friday, to be a half owner of a thriving business in one of the wealthiest areas of the country. Things like this didn't happen to people like her; this was the stuff of holiday reading.

What would her mum and her gran say? She knew exactly what her dad would say. It would be along the lines of, 'Well done, lass. I'm sure you've earned every penny. I'm right proud of thee.'

Her mum would probably say, 'Well, lass, time you and me had a holiday together.'

Her gran would be packed and asking to borrow the train fare to come and be looked after for the rest of her days saying, 'I always had a soft spot for you, love. I always knew you'd do well.'

Her life would never be the same again. It had been flipped on its head. What she couldn't understand was how something as enormous as this could happen to her, while all around life was going on as normal, as if nothing had changed.

Shop windows were being cleaned by a window cleaner, the post was being collected by a post man, the promenade was being swept, ice creams were being licked, coffees drunk, cigarettes smoked and kids shouted at. Nothing had changed in the whole world, except she had just inherited close to £400,000.

What was tormenting her was whether to tell Joanne.

Why was she even contemplating not telling Joanne? She was her best friend. Was it because she didn't trust her, or was it because Joanne's business was doing so well that she was considering employing a manager and soon wouldn't be needed at the funeral parlour more than a day a week?

Veronica knew Joanne would become bored very quickly if she was at home every day and would refocus on another challenge. Formally linking her funeral business with Veronica's care home would be seen as a very lucrative, backward integration, business strategy.

Veronica envisaged Joanne meekly offering to take some of the onerous financial complications of running a business away from her. 'Just until you get your feet under the table, you understand,' she would say.

Veronica would feel changes creeping into her care home behind her back. Residents would be rehoused statistically in order of life expectancy. Those most likely to depart this world sooner rather than later would be encouraged to move into ground floor accommodation, for the convenience of staff and also for the convenience of Vincent and his collection team.

For new inmates, DNR (Do Not Resuscitate) paperwork would need to be automatically completed on arrival and duly signed by the family, just as a formality. Routinely, everyone would be enlisted into The Club.

Or perhaps it was because she might be pressurised by Joanne to sell her half of the care home, regardless of the consequences to Godfrey or Miss Tan. If she did that she would be no better than any of the folk at the reading of Miss Violet Ann's will.

Veronica shuddered at the thought. Godfrey's words came into her mind when he recounted Joanne's reaction as he was opening the safe, 'Joanne was almost salivating with the thoughts of riches and wealth. Her eyes became narrow, dilated and focussed.'

It was becoming a little cold and Veronica shivered as she sat on the bench thinking. What would she have done twelve months ago?

She smiled to herself for she would have, without hesitation, rushed into the nearest supermarket with a trolley and run through the alcohol aisles, filling it to overflowing with champagne, gin, vodka, red wine, white wine, crisps and finger food. Maybe she would have remembered to put in a few tonics. Then, she would have run with the loaded trolley all the way to Joanne's office, regardless of who was there, burst in and insisted upon opening champagne for everyone and partying until she couldn't stand.

No, now it was for real. Now there wasn't just her to consider. Now there were Miss Tan and Godfrey, not forgetting all the other residents. Now there was too much at stake to be frivolous.

Veronica decided to say nothing, just for the moment.

Perhaps she had just become an adult.

21

The deeds of the five run-down properties on the promenade were set out on the solicitor's desk.

"I'm afraid to say, Mrs Wendover, that when your late husband, Mr Gordon Wendover, acquired these properties, he omitted to complete a number of legally binding documents such as registering the purchases with the land registry. In the absence of registry submissions, the local authority has been making extensive enquiries through the local and national press to find the current owner. Now they have found the current owner, they can proceed by serving compulsory purchase orders on the properties as part of a major development for the town."

Joanne listened without interruption, for once.

"We will, of course, contest this but they can proceed under The Power of Eminent Domain for they have a very good public interest case. The site is required for a prestigious, new, seafront development, and the complete row of virtually derelict properties will be demolished. Unfortunately, there is little we can do about it now but we will try. You will, of course, get the compulsory purchase price known as condemnation, but I know it is well down on the realistic price. Hopefully, you will see £70,000 for each property as some compensation."

Joanne winced at the thought of losing the true value of the properties, but consoled herself in the thought that, until recently, she knew nothing about the contents of the safe. £350,000 in hand, minus inheritance tax, will do nicely, she thought.

"Thank you, Gordon," she whispered to herself. "Perhaps you weren't such a bastard after all."

On her way back to her office, she stopped off for a coffee and a cake and found herself pondering whether she should tell Veronica about her windfall.

After some consideration she believed she knew what Veronica would want to do. Veronica would want to try and drink the town dry that night, starting at one end and not stopping until they were at the other end, then she would want to give up work immediately and for the two of them to holiday in Spain for months.

No, on reflection she would keep her windfall to herself for the time being. Joanne paid for the coffee and cake and walked the short distance to the funeral parlour.

Back in her office, she roughly pushed Humphrey the cat off the pile of CVs on her desk. There was no love lost between the pair and Humphrey resented the intrusion into his afternoon nap, settling down again on the opposite corner of her desk and eyeing her through green slits.

He then started to display his displeasure in his inimitable style. First a slight cough. Then a series of choking sounds.

Then the sound of retching coming from deep down in his stomach, followed by silence.

Has his tantrum finished, Joanne wondered? When replaying what normally happened with the cat at this juncture, she suddenly remembered he'd caught her out by this silent ruse before. She jumped up, caught the protesting cat by the scruff of his neck and ran with him towards her closed office door.

Too late.

Before she had time to fully open the door, an enormous fur ball splatted right in the centre of the mustard coloured, leather, button-backed, antique chair positioned beside the door. The evil looking mix of fur, spittle and bile slid down the leatherwork, hanging like wet tennis shoelaces.

Experience had taught Joanne that this was not the end of the ordeal so, quick as lightning, she spun the cat around and threw him backwards into the corridor through the open door. In mid-air, part two of Humphrey's displeasure gun fired from his rear end just as she slammed the door shut.

"Result!" exclaimed Joanne and punched the air, imagining the area of stained wallpaper slowly peeling off the corridor wall from the ghastly, gaseous onslaught. Joanne then pushed the soiled mustard chair out into the corridor and slammed the door shut once more.

She settled down in the still sweet-smelling room, congratulating herself on avoiding having to open all the windows and evacuate the room for a full thirty minutes while the cat's flatulence dissipated.

Joanne really did hate the cat. Once or twice Joanne had

spotted the cat ambling across the drive while she had been reversing her car, and had accelerated but missed. Next time, she had promised herself. Next time.

She turned her attention to the matter in hand. Joanne set about examining the pile of uncensored CVs recently sent from the local newspaper. She quickly despaired for they read like a list of the nearly dead.

She put her head in her hands and sighed. There wasn't a spark of life in any of them. Not a flicker of enthusiasm for the job; no fervour, no eagerness, not a trace of passion about anything. How difficult could it be to find a manager?

To widen the net even further, she had suggested that experience in the funeral sector was not necessary. If the candidate had run a business before, had regular contact with the public, and had managed staff and suppliers, he or she would be considered.

Originally, she had been a little excited by the task and had been looking forward to reading the CVs. She was expecting the job of paring down the list of potentials to challenge her, rather than having to hunt for vaguely possible candidates. An early set of interviews was not to be.

The full range of CV presentations were spread out on her desk. They ranged from beautiful, copperplate handwriting to a badly torn out page of an exercise book.

She read on in disbelief, becoming even more disillusioned. Many of the CVs were peppered with grammatical and spelling errors, making them virtually incomprehensible.

I have been a exemplory manger for twelve year's working on a farme.

I am a manager with strong breath of...

Marital status: desperate!

Non-work related interests: cooking people and animals.

The final straw was when someone cited God as a reference and named all twelve of her pets!

Joanne swept the whole lot into the bin and wrote another job advert, to a wider range of newspapers, concluding with *previous applicants need not apply*.

Two weeks later, she groaned as she sat down to examine a second pile of applicants. "Change your mind set," she chided herself. "In here will be a diamond of a manager who will take the business to new heights because I'm getting a little bit bored with it."

She started reading the first CV. Half way down the first page she said out loud, "Bin."

Next CV. "Bin."

Her head was already sinking into her hands. "Here we bloody well go again."

"Aha. Well now, what have we here?" she asked, perking up. "You may just be a possible, Staff Sergeant Gareth Alfred Garington. Ex-army, just demobbed, lives nearby. Been on PR duties for the Army for the last five years. Let's give you a go." She put his CV to one side.

On reflection, she couldn't say whether it was the poor quality of the other candidates, or the Army and other entries on his CV that interested her, probably because she'd always been a sucker for a man in uniform.

Next CV. "Bin."

Next CV. "Bin."

The bin was already overflowing.

Then she became excited. The second potential candidate was a serving funeral parlour manager with plenty of experience, who was currently working for a local competitor. She had heard good reports of Mr Denis Alan Chetwyn.

Anyway, even if he wasn't any good, she would take the opportunity to find out about the enemy. It might even lead to a takeover. That will be fun, she mused.

Next CV. "Bin. Some of these are worse than the last lot!"

She needed at least three to interview; just one more to find.

"Peter James White." She read aloud from his CV. "Been the manager of a small engineering business, increased the turnover by 50% in two years, regularly dealt with the public, suppliers and customers. Needs a new challenge." Seems OK. Better than most I've read today, she thought. "Hobbies include football, cycling and swimming. Oh no, a bloody fitness freak! That's all I need around here, but needs must when the devil rides."

Next CV. "Bin."

Last CV. "Bin."

Job done. Interview invitations were sent out that day. One thing that could be said about Joanne was when she had made up her mind, she really moved on it. That's when folk struggled to keep up.

22

Contrary to her normal, solitary way of doing things, Joanne decided to enlist the assistance of Veronica and Vincent.

Her own role would be to chair the interviews using her knowledge of the business world, Vincent would be there for his sector specific knowledge to assess whether the candidates were telling the truth, and Veronica...well, Veronica was there to...to make up the numbers.

Elsie showed the first candidate, Staff Sergeant Gareth Garington, into Joanne's office. He stood ramrod straight behind the chair and stretched out his hand to shake Joanne's, then Veronica's, then Vincent's. He was patiently waiting to be invited to sit down.

Before Elsie left, she asked if he would like a cup of tea to make him feel more comfortable. He smiled and thanked her saying, "Milk and four sugars please!"

He was a smart, short, well-groomed man who seemed to be wearing what was fashionable when he first went into the Army thirty years ago. Highly polished toe-capped shoes, trousers with razor sharp creases and turn-ups, a crisp white shirt, a strange, brightly coloured tartan tie, and a tweed jacket.

Joanne sat between the other interviewers and proceeded to ask the first question, as practised beforehand. "So, Gareth, tell us about yourself."

Born in London and grown up in the docklands, Gareth said he had joined the Army as soon as he could when he was sixteen.

A litany of postings followed, demonstrating he had been to every area of unrest in the world for the last thirty years. He went on to say that it was now time for him to settle down and get a civvie job.

"What do you think has been your greatest achievement?" asked Veronica, uncharacteristically sticking to the script.

He suddenly became animated, now in his familiar world. "Well, Miss, that's an easy one. We was out in the middle-east, you know, sand everywhere, when me and my mates was attacked by a 'orde of the enemy. We was surrounded, there seemed to be 'undreds of them, lead wasps flying everywhere, I mean bullets. We tried to call for back up but the radio was dead! We was well and truly fu... sorry, Miss, in trouble. Night was drawing in and under cover of darkness we knew what the enemy would do. They would creep in and slit our throats from ear to ear.' He demonstrated the action. "We wouldn't know nufink about it."

Joanne looked away.

"We couldn't just sit there, could we? We had to do somefink, so me and Mickey Dripping, on account of him being a useless plumber before he joined the mob, decided to set fire to the brush 'cos the wind was in the right direction. Soon we had a proper Guy Fawkes bonfire going and it spread to all the surrounding fields where the enemy was hiding. They started running for cover and we shot 'em all, all twenty one."

Gareth's excited hands were demonstrating the fire spreading across the fields, then he fired his pretend rifle very realistically several times, even down to the recoil.

"And were you a hero for that?"

"With the Army we was all 'eroes, but we inadvertently set fire to two opium farms next to the scrub and the farmers chased me and my squad all the way back to the barracks. They'd 'ave been worse than the enemy if they'd caught up with us. They would 'ave-"

"Yes, yes, well, thank you for recounting that. Is there anything you would like to ask us about the job of funeral parlour manager?" interrupted Joanne, keen to move on.

"No, Miss, I'm OK with the dead. Seen 'undreds of them I 'ave. Theirs and ours, shot to bits, run over, drowned, killed by friendly fire, seen 'em all I 'ave."

"Thank you. We'll be in touch."

When he was out of the room Joanne groaned and said, "A definite no!"

Vincent also said a definite, "No!"

And Veronica suggested they couldn't afford the sugar.

So much for a man in uniform, mused Joanne. "Next?"

Denis Alan Chetwyn was next. He was an experienced

funeral director from the local competition. He was smart, spoke very good English, and was courteous.

He answered every one of Vincent's questions well and, when asked if he had any questions, proceeded to want to know all the details about the parlour. He wanted to know the turnover, the finances, the profit and loss, and the accounts procedures.

Joanne wasn't having any of that so hedged all the questions, realising that contrary to her plan to find out about the competition's parlour, Denis had been sent to find out about her parlour. She answered vaguely, giving nothing away, but following the agreed format of the interview to the letter. Then she asked when he could start.

That took him aback.

It also took Veronica and Vincent aback.

He mumbled, "Say, four weeks?"

Then she offered him the job! There and then, with a 20% increase in his current salary, and a car!

Veronica was stunned. Vincent's mouth dropped open and when he suggested they shouldn't be too hasty, Joanne banged the table and announced, "Decision made. Do you want the job?"

Denis Chetwyn agreed to take the job, agreed to start in one month, and shook Joanne's hand. He left the room dumfounded.

As soon as he was out Veronica started. "So, precisely what was my role in all this, was I here just to make up the numbers? You might as well have dragged two corpses in from the little fridge for all the bloody use Vincent and I have been. And Vincent, well, he could have been doing something much more useful like polishing the inside of his exhaust pipe, or whatever it is he does in the garage all day. What a complete bloody waste of my time this has been. I'm off, there's no point interviewing the last one because there's no job now."

They both rose from their seats.

"Sit down, Veronica, and you too, Vincent. I'm not seriously offering him the job. He's not for us. I wouldn't trust him an inch. Anyone who would sneak into a competitor's premises under the false pretence of looking for a job deserves all he gets. I'll give him a week to put his notice in, then another week to consolidate his position of leaving, and then tell him that I've changed my mind for some operational reason. His boss will be furious with us for trying to poach Denis. That was never his underhanded plan. Despite being let down by me, Denis will believe he is worth far more than he is being paid by his current boss and will ask for a big, fat, wage rise and a car, or threaten to leave. Everyone will be angry. Hopefully, we have just disrupted their whole business for a long time."

There was a silence while the other two caught up.

"You devious bitch," said Veronica.

Vincent winced at Joanne's cold heartedness and made a mental note to himself to be careful of this boss.

"Don't you sanctimonious pair ever forget it's dog eat dog in the commercial world out there, and it's only the lead Husky who has the best view. I intend to be the lead Husky in funerals in this area."

Elsie led the next candidate into Joanne's office and asked if he wanted a cup of tea. The three interviewers were busy reading the final candidate's CV and didn't even look up.

Peter James White replied loudly, "No thank you. I'd rather have a large Sex on the Beach please."

Joanne was first to look up. She smiled widely and her eyes became misty.

Veronica looked up next and immediately took Vincent's arm, suggesting they should leave, explaining that Joanne could probably conduct this interview on her own.

Vincent, by now, had come to accept the strange goings on and obediently allowed himself to be led out of the office, gently closing the door behind them.

When they were alone, Joanne went around the table and hesitantly approached Daz.

"I'm so, so pleased to see you again," she mumbled.

"Me, too."

"No, I really am."

"I wasn't sure how I would be received. If you might be in a special relationship now and I would just be an embarrassment."

"No, not at all, not at all. I'm really thrilled you came."

He held both his hands out and took both of hers. Moving closer, they put their cheeks together, delighting in the touch and feel. Nothing had changed. Then they kissed. It started hesitantly enough but soon became the same kiss as the last time they were together.

Immediately spirited back to the Spanish beach, Joanne

could hear the gentle cymbals of the sea as the tiny Mediterranean waves fell rhythmically upon the shore. She could feel the fine sand between her toes and smell the clumps of turtle-cropped, shredded seaweed along the beach. It was wonderful.

As they held on to each other, not saying a word, memories of sitting on the beach watching the big, red sun sink down towards the sea flooded back. Joanne remembered Daz making a hissing sound as the waning sun on the far-off horizon first touched the water.

Then reality kicked in for Joanne. She stood back and looked him full in the face.

"Daz! What the hell are you doing here?"

"I've come for the funeral parlour manager's job. Seriously, I'd like to be considered for the job."

Joanne shook her racing head.

Chuckling to herself, Veronica quickly moved away from Joanne's closed office door.

23

There is never a right time to leave this world but one evening, after a particularly painful day, Miss Tan did leave. Peacefully, and with Godfrey and Veronica at her side, Miss Tan slipped from this life into the next. With just a squeeze of her hand she said goodbye, left the pain behind, and became whole again ready for her next adventure. Veronica and Godfrey both cried.

Three weeks later, the church bell sounded across the sleepy village, urging people to come to the funeral of Charlotte Ann Wendover, or Miss Tan as she was better known to everyone in the village, and celebrate her life.

It was a cheerful bell, a friendly sound inviting folk to come and sing praises, to remember her with fondness and joy, and to share memories of her contribution to the village. A bell that encouraged people to rejoice.

Those who had been to her Sunday School as children, and sat at her feet in a silent circle listening to her engaging versions of bible stories with eyes opened wide, knew Miss

Tan had influenced their lives. They, in turn, were now passing on that learning to their children.

Whenever anyone spoke of Miss Tan, they spoke with a fondness tinged with regret that such pain attended her last years.

Veronica wondered, as she walked towards the little church, how the same bell could sound so different. Not many weeks ago she had walked to the church for Violet Ann's funeral, listening to a mournful bell. A sorrowful sound, announcing the end of an unhappy life; the final toll, the closing of a sad, sad book.

Whereas today, the same, old, familiar, cracked bell seemed almost happy. It seemed to be saying it was a privilege to have been chosen, out of the scores of bells in the locality, to announce to the world not that Miss Tan had gone, but rather to celebrate that Miss Tan had arrived!

As she walked in the sunshine, Veronica wondered if the tenor of the bell could be influenced by the bell ringer's demeanour. At Miss Violet Ann's funeral, the indifferent vicar had tolled the bell himself. His matter-of-fact, just a job attitude had travelled up the rope and influenced its message: Come if you must, it won't matter whether you are here or not, it's just a process to be gone through, I'm not paid enough to be here for very long, so be quick.

But today, there was a different vicar on the end of the bell rope. It was a kindly, old vicar who had been brought out of retirement especially for today. The same kindly, old vicar who tended the churchyard with such care and placed fresh, wild flowers on the graves of those departed. The bell tolled kindness, fondness and love.

When her death was imminent, Miss Tan set out the whole

ceremony with Veronica and Godfrey, specifically asking if the old vicar, who she had known since she had been a little girl, would take the service.

She had no idea the request would spark off such an ecumenical war. The incumbent vicar had apoplexy at the thought of another vicar presiding over Miss Tan's funeral. Particularly a retired vicar who was so well liked in the village. A vicar whose parishioners took every opportunity to recount the sensitive ways he used to do things before the incumbent vicar came to post.

The situation hadn't been helped by Joanne who, in her inimitable way of organising the funeral, had coldly announced the swap to him and he had exploded.

Puffed up and standing at a full five feet four inches in his built-up shoes, he had pompously announced, "I am appointed to vicariously officiate at all services in this church on behalf of his eminence the bishop. As such, I will decide who officiates and who does not in my church. Not you!"

"I'm paying so the old vicar does the funeral ceremony," Joanne had snapped.

"Not in my church!" the vicar had shouted, the colour in his cheeks deepening.

"Then I'll write to the bishop and get you moved!" Joanne had blasted.

He had dismissed the threat with, "In your dreams."

Joanne, not to be undermined by a vicar, had moved to a lower level of combat. "And I'll mention to the bishop that you claim funeral fees for a bell ringer and a church warden, but I've never seen either and you do all the jobs yourself!"

There was a slight hesitation at this latest salvo from Joanne as the vicar considered the consequences, but he had continued, red-faced. "You can do your worst, Madam, because I'm officiating at the funeral." He had started to walk away from the onslaught.

Joanne had shouted after him, "This will be the last funeral you get in this church as long as I'm running the funeral parlour then!"

"Whatever!"

A complete impasse had been reached between the two.

Joanne reported back to Veronica that the vicar was being a complete arse and wouldn't allow the old vicar to officiate.

"You didn't upset him, did you?" asked a knowing Veronica.

"Certainly not. He's just an intransigent vicar with Napoleon syndrome, but I'm not sure he'll change his mind."

Veronica knew she would be starting a conversation with the vicar from a very weak position now that Joanne had stirred things up. Despite what Joanne had said, Veronica knew the discussion would have become progressively more vitriolic, and Joanne would have driven him into a corner where he would have had no option but to stamp his foot and say, "No."

Veronica believed the chat she was about to have with him would be like trying to snuggle up to an angry wasp. She invited him to meet her for afternoon tea and cakes at the best tea shop around.

When he was awash with tea and full of smoked salmon and cucumber sandwiches (with the crusts cut off), followed by Battenberg and fondant fancies, she mentioned that Miss Tan had asked specifically if the incumbent vicar would say a prayer at her wake.

Veronica watched the incumbent vicar's eyes light up at the word wake, wondering if he was already planning how to arrange one more carrier bag under his cassock.

The vicar pondered. Another fairy cake disappeared. Time to strike. Veronica went on to say Miss Tan had asked if he would take on the onerous roll of disposing of all the leftover food from the wake and distributing it as he saw fit. The incumbent vicar was now on the edge. Nearly there, Veronica thought.

"Oh, and there was one other thing. Miss Tan asked if she could make a donation to the church, through you, to allow the old vicar to preside over proceedings."

Job done! Change his mind she did. Where there's avarice there's always a way, Veronica mused.

The old, retired vicar had tears in his eyes when asked if he would preside over the service by Veronica. Miss Tan had served his Sunday School faithfully, for so many years, and all the children loved her. He said there was nobody else in the world he would rather do it for. He didn't need to do any research for he already had years of happy memories at his fingertips. He would consider it a privilege.

When Veronica arrived at the church there was already a huge crowd gathered, all waiting respectfully outside.

The old hearse whispered to a standstill at the lychgate, and Vincent and his casket-bearers, as one, moved into position. The casket was specially made of hazel branches, and the congregation parted to allow the casket through. Silently, they followed into the church.

Inside, everyone was given a yellow rose, with an attached luggage label to write a message to Miss Tan. Everyone was asked to leave the rose near the altar when Miss Tan went out for the interment. Miss Tan's thinking was that as Godfrey couldn't be there for the funeral, he could at least read all the messages when the mourners departed and he was alone.

The service was the best funeral service anyone could remember. Posies of wild flowers were attached to every pew end and bouquets were placed upon the hazel casket.

The congregation consisted of about sixty ex-Sunday school children, young mums, the W.I., members of the choir, and all who had received a kindness from Miss Tan in their life time.

The hymn All Things Bright and Beautiful was so poignant it made everyone cry, and the sermon was alive and full of joy. Had Miss Tan been there, she couldn't have been happier.

The old vicar recounted tales of Miss Tan's mischief as a youngster and her contribution to the village and the Sunday school. Many times, he had the congregation laughing. It was as close to a perfect send off as they come. Veronica was so pleased.

Godfrey was there too, innocuously disguised in gardening clothes and a beanie hat, busying himself cutting the hedge close to the main door. Veronica had deliberately left it open for him to hear the service and the singing.

When everyone was inside, he perched himself on a

headstone near the door and participated in the singing and the service.

For the interment, he busied himself collecting fallen branches on the other side of a nearby wall. It was the best Veronica could arrange under the circumstances.

When all the mourners had left the site of the interment, Godfrey had a small service of his own and said his tearful goodbye to his beautiful wife and soulmate. He placed a dozen red roses carefully on her casket in the grave.

After the wake, Veronica made her way back to be with Godfrey. Although he had seen and heard the service and the internment, attending the wake was far too risky.

Veronica was able to fill in all the gaps, especially the antics of the incumbent vicar who tried to balance three overflowing carrier bags of Elsie's sandwiches and cakes on the handles of his bicycle before cycling home.

Together in Miss Tan's bedroom, they read the messages on the yellow rose luggage labels. After a while they both had to stop as the written memories became just too painful. Veronica left, went home and cried herself to sleep.

Two days later, she called in to see Godfrey. Over a cup of tea she asked him bluntly, "What now for you?"

"Don't know," he sighed. "Life's impossible without papers. Stay here until I go to join Tan, I suppose."

"Is that what she would have wanted?"

"Probably not, but what's the alternative?"

"There are about a million people out there who are making a living working in the UK without any papers, so why not you? Make a new life for yourself somewhere. You're OK for money, aren't you?"

"Money's not a problem. The funeral parlour deliveries paid me well, and Tan made sure I had plenty of cash to see me through."

They toasted Tan together and gave each other a hug.

Veronica left Godfrey to his thoughts.

24

Daz and Joanne rarely left each other's sides for the first few days of his stay.

Veronica thought it was a pleasure to see Joanne with a smile on her face and a rosy glow about her as she worked.

While Joanne was still considering whether to offer Daz the manager's job, he took on the tasks and responsibilities with a professionalism which did not surprise either Joanne or Veronica.

Joanne, although falling in love, was savvy enough to know that a holiday romance was not a good basis for a business relationship, but she was getting to know a little more about him each day.

When he was close he excited her and she needed to touch him. He, in turn, was delighted to be back with her, but also realised that their Spanish fling was not a basis for working together either.

However, love dumbs the brain sometimes and before Veronica could intervene with some grounded common sense, Joanne had indeed set Daz up as the funeral parlour manager. What Veronica was able to do, in one of Joanne's more sensible moments, was to ensure she insisted on a long probation period.

Veronica continued with her advice. "If you want a partner in the business world Jo Jo, get a dog!" She was trying to talk some sense into Joanne.

"I don't want a partner; I want a manager."

"A manager you sleep with as a partner?"

"Don't be coarse."

"Jo Jo, you're really not the easiest person to get on with. Sometimes you can be as prickly as a conker shell, and other times as smooth as silk. You're usually trying to do the right thing, but often you approach people in the wrong way. I'm used to you now and take no notice, but you can really hack folk off by the way you go about some things."

"What, me? How on earth do I hack people off?"

"You have a way. You don't mean it, but you do."

"Who have I hacked off recently, then? Go on, tell me?"

"OK, then, how about the vicar?"

"Oh, he was just an arse. What about here in the parlour?"

"Oh, I don't know. Say you did something here in the funeral parlour that was the equivalent to locking your new manager, Daz, in your car boot, and you also locked your dog in the boot. Who would be wagging their tail and still want to be your friend when you let them out? The dog every time! You don't seem to realise that people don't forget or forgive when you hack them off. At best, they don't trust you again and don't put 100% into your business. At worst, they wait to get their own back. I think Daz will be gone within six months."

"You really do have a queer way of looking at things, Veronica, and I've still got that bloody useless lump of cat Gordon left me. I don't need a dog as well."

Humphrey was in his usual spot on the corner of her spacious desk. He was lying down preening himself, with one back leg high in the air as he licked his nether region.

Veronica looked on in amazement at the old cat's agility and suppleness, completely mesmerised. She said absently, "I wish I could do that, Jo Jo!"

Without looking up from her papers Joanne replied, "Throw him a fishy titbit and he'll let you!"

To be fair to Daz, he took the role really seriously, sitting down with Vincent and with Elsie for days at a time, asking question after question about the funeral business. He wasn't frightened by Elsie's role and wore a long, rubber apron alongside her on occasion.

They warmed to him, being so unlike their current, cold, scheming boss. He was there early to open up, and usually left late.

Joanne spent quality time introducing him to some, although not all, of the movements of money in the funeral business. Due to his business studies college course, he absorbed things quickly.

With recently bereaved clients, Daz had warmth and empathy beyond his years. He was good with the recently widowed, great with children under their harrowing circumstance, and treated recent widowers with understanding.

He's going to make a good funeral parlour manager, thought Joanne.

Once the appointment had been announced, she decided it was time for him to move into the funeral parlour's second flat. However, as Veronica was still living there the conversation was going to be a difficult one.

Joanne decided to broach the subject with her after a few gins that Saturday night.

"You know how you've said you feel uncomfortable being here in the funeral parlour flat alone at night? That it's really spooky? Well, I've seen a smashing modern flat in the town with a Juliette balcony, a tiny garden, and a garage for your car. It's in a very quiet cul-de-sac populated by other professional people like you," said Joanne, laying on the flattery. "Of course, you'd still always be welcome here as often as you'd like and we'd still have our Saturday nights together, wouldn't we? What do you say?"

"You need to know," said the slightly braver Veronica, awash with gin, "that the flat in town doesn't appeal at all."

Joanne was about to jump in with another hundred convincing reasons why it would be a good idea when Veronica shushed her. "I have the option to move into the Bethesda Care Home. To take a flat there - all meals and bills paid for, and any odd jobs would be done for me free of charge."

"Wouldn't that still cost a fortune? I'll bet there'll be dozens of hidden costs."

"No, none."

"How's that?"

"I own the Bethesda Care Home now."

"What? You own the Care Home? All of it? Why didn't you tell me? That's fantastic! It must be worth a small fortune. Are we going to sell it?"

"No, *we* are not going to sell it. I'm going to run it as the best care home on the south coast."

There was a long pause as Joanne topped up the peanuts. "When were you going to tell me?"

"When you were full of gin, like tonight."

There was a long pause before Veronica, who up until then had been genuinely embarrassed that she had not told Joanne about the care home, decided to level the playing field.

"So, how are the sales of the big houses on the prom going? Have you sold any yet?"

Joanne looked up, uncomfortable by the sudden question. "I was going to tell you."

"Tell me what?"

"About the progress with the houses."

"When?"

"When you were full of gin, like tonight."

"Are *we* going to sell them, then?"

"No. I've already received the money from the council's compulsory purchase order."

"When were you going to tell me you'd had all the money?"

"Another drink?" asked Joanne.

Veronica moved out of her funeral parlour flat a month later, and into her Bethesda Care Home flat. Miss Tan had been equally as generous as Miss Violet Ann in bequeathing her the remainder of the ownership of the Bethesda Care Home for all her friendship and service, on the promise that Godfrey could stay on in Miss Tan's suite for as long as he wanted.

Veronica had Miss Violet Ann's suite decorated and completely refurnished for herself, and her lounge looked out over the pristine gardens.

As soon as her ownership was announced, Veronica called a meeting with all the staff. She told them that she now owned Bethesda Care Home, and her plans were to make it the very best care home on the south coast.

Champagne for everyone toasted their combined future and her target. The staff were thrilled Veronica was going to stay on for many had worked with her. They loved her humour and the understanding she brought to caring for the elderly and infirm. They had been expecting a much worse outcome.

Veronica asked the care home manager if she would stay on, and was delighted when she said yes.

However, Nurse Rosalind, who was *still* off sick, had to go!

25

The funeral parlour was doing well. The Bethesda Care Home was doing well. The Victorian and Georgian coins were being disposed of in a regulated manner. The properties on the prom had all but been demolished. The deliveries were continuing on a regular basis, although not at their previous rate. The only thing left to be dealt with was the Torah Finial Bells.

One particular Saturday night, Veronica invited Joanne and Daz over to her suite in the care home. The gin flowed as it had always flowed, but the quality of the food went way above the previous value pasta, offer price pizzas, and jumbo bags of crisps.

During the evening, the conversation drifted around the events in the two businesses over the last week, eventually settling on what was to be done with the Torah Finial Bells.

After a short explanation to Daz, obviously missing out the Godfrey connection, Joanne sheepishly announced she had already arranged to put them up for auction in London in a week's time.

Veronica snapped. "That wasn't the plan. We all agreed we would talk about their future together. One of the suggestions was to return the bells to their original owner, remember?"

"Have you any idea what they could be worth?" asked the incredulous Joanne.

"Nothing compared with what they would be worth to their original owners, or to whole communities, after all this time," Veronica bounced back.

"But we don't know who the original owners are. We haven't a clue. We've no idea what country they originated from, we've no idea if they are even Jewish, and we've no idea how Godfrey acquired them, or even if they are his. Have you thought he might have been keeping them safe for their true owners before you go off and give them to someone else?" Joanne argued.

"We don't know who owns them because we haven't tried to find the owners and you're about to flog them off to the highest bidder," Veronica hollered.

"Where would we start? The owners could be anywhere. Probably all dead by now!" Joanne's volume was rising.

"I've no idea, but we ought to start somewhere," shouted back Veronica.

The argument raged noisily between the cousins for over half an hour, back and forth, back and forth, both getting crosser by the moment, before Daz innocently interjected and immediately wished he hadn't.

"How about this then, Jo Jo? Veronica tries to find the owner and if that fails in the next three months, then you put them up for auction?"

"Shut up, Daz. You don't have the foggiest idea what you're talking about!"

"Steady on, Jo Jo. I was only trying to help. I thought it a good compromise."

"Well it's not. It's a stupid idea. Just keep right out of it. I don't need your help. And stop calling me bloody Jo Jo," snapped Joanne.

Daz was ready for a fight too, but thought better of it. "I think I'll just make my own way home." With that, he rose to go, naively half expecting an apology. There was none.

"Suit yourself," Joanne barked.

The door closed quietly behind him.

The tense atmosphere was broken a few minutes later when Godfrey knocked.

"Sorry, but I couldn't help but overhear the conversation. In fact, most of the residents will probably have heard."

"Well, tough. They'd prefer to hear that than be bloody deaf!" snapped Joanne.

"Hold on a minute, Joanne, these are my residents and I actually like most of them," said Veronica.

Rising to leave Joanne asked, in a more placatory manner, "Godfrey, will you come around on Friday to open the safe for me? The security company is coming to take the bell things to London on Saturday for a Monday auction."

"Of course, I will. I have a few things to do during the day, but I'll be there when everyone has gone home at about 7.30 pm if that's all right? I'm sure Veronica will take me."

Without saying anything, Veronica went noisily off to the kitchen in a real strop.

The door closed behind Joanne as she left without saying goodbye.

As soon as Joanne was gone, Veronica bounced out of the kitchen back into the lounge, angry and hurt. She handed Godfrey a drink.

"Godfrey, how could you agree to do that?"

"Easy, I've had lots of practice with the cantankerous old safe. I'd actually be quite good as a safe breaker, what do you think?" he held up his fingers, examining them to tease her.

"You know exactly what I mean. I thought you agreed with me that we needed to at least try and locate the owners."

"I still do."

"So why agree to open the safe for her on Friday?"

"Because it's empty," Godfrey said, having another sip of his gin and tonic.

"What do you mean, it's empty?" queried Veronica.

"Yep, empty as a pauper's larder. I heard Joanne say she was going to auction the bells on Monday so whilst you were shouting and arguing I borrowed your car - I hope you don't mind – drove over to the parlour, and took them out of the safe. They're in my flat. You and I have just six days to find the original owners."

"Well, you wily old fox. Top up?"

"Yes, another very large one please."

Back in the funeral parlour there was a note left pinned to Joanne's door.

To Jo Jo,

Thanks for the ace time in Spain, and thanks for the offer of the job here at the funeral parlour. I think the job would have been very challenging, however, not as challenging as being with a woman who, as I have witnessed on several occasions, speaks to her amazing staff with as little respect as you do. The last straw for me was how you spoke to me tonight in front of Veronica. I don't believe you will ever change, and I won't ever accept it, so better we part now.

I won't forget Spain. It was, as I said, ace. We should have left it there as a lovely memory. I'll try to forget the rest.

Daz

After reading the note Joanne screwed it up and threw it fiercely into the corner of her lounge. In a huff, she poured herself a big drink and sat down.

Suddenly, unfamiliar tears rolled down her face, plopping into her balloon glass one after the other, melting the ice.

26

The next morning, after Veronica and Joanne's spat, Veronica and Godfrey sat down to try to work out what to do.

"Six days? What can we do in only six days? Where on earth will we start?" pondered Veronica.

"We start with all the assumptions, the hopes and clues we have. The first assumption is that the artefacts are Jewish. The second is that they came from the continent. The hope is that there are some folk left who can remember them. The first and only real clue is in the form of three, torn, return bus tickets I found at the bottom of the box. They are all for a local return journey, from a town with an unreadable name to Santander in northern Spain. So, we have lots to go on," encouraged Godfrey.

"Is that it? Not much is it? I'm not going to be much help when it comes to geography. All I know is Spain is a long way off the end of the runway at Heathrow."

"It's more than we had yesterday. Oh, and we have the Torah Finial Bells in our possession."

"True. But on Friday when you don't turn up, Joanne will know we have them because you are the only person who can open the safe. I'm not sure what she'll do when there's such an enormous amount of money at stake. She's capable of anything when she gets focussed."

"True, so you and I need to get over to Santander in northern Spain to start the search."

"I love your optimism, Godfrey, but aren't you forgetting something? No papers? How will you possibly get through passport control without all the alarms going off? You can't go and I can't go on my own because I can get lost in a loo."

"But I speak German and French and you speak...?" he asked.

"A lot," Veronica admitted.

"So, the problem is twofold. Number one, we need to get across the channel in a vehicle that I can hide in. Number two, we need to smuggle religious artefacts into Spain. I think both will command a hefty jail sentence if we are caught."

"No problem then. And where would you like me to magic up a lorry from at short notice?" asked a sarcastic Veronica.

"I don't know. Maybe you know someone who has such a vehicle and would let us use it?"

"Let's just have a moment of reality, shall we? You want me to hire or borrow a big vehicle and transport stolen Jewish artefacts across Europe with a hidden, stateless person in the back of the vehicle? Is that it? Have I understood you correctly?"

"Well, yes."

"Then only two little things are worrying me. One, I don't actually have a licence to drive. I never quite got around to taking my test all those years ago; it all seemed like a lot of bother. And two, I can only drive little cars because I bump bigger ones into things...a lot."

"What? You don't have a licence?"

"Not yet."

Godfrey shook his head in disbelief. "Who do you know who has such a vehicle, can drive, and has a licence?"

"Nobody. Aha, but hang on, I've just had a thought. We're going for a spin."

At the car Godfrey hesitated. "Should I be worried, getting in a car driven by a lady who doesn't possess a driving licence?"

"Just shut up and get in," Veronica replied.

That afternoon Veronica and Godfrey found themselves calling at a hardware shop further along the coast. The manager of the shop explained that the owners had sold the business to him recently but, as far as he was aware, they still lived locally. He kindly passed on their home address.

Veronica drove to the address, knocked, stood back and waited.

Rosie flung her arms around Veronica's neck as soon as she saw who it was. "Oh, I'm so pleased to see you! I did try to find you after the holiday, but the holiday company wouldn't release any addresses. What are you doing here? I was so sorry when we lost touch. Come in, come in. We did have such fun in Spain, didn't we? I've only just recovered from that hangover! Was I rough? How's Joanne?"

"She's fine and living on the south coast. Where's Christopher?"

Rosie looked at the kitchen door as it opened and in came, not Christopher, but the dream of a waiter from their hotel. "I think you know Alejandro?" she said with a smirk.

"Rosie!" exclaimed Veronica out loud. "You tart!" She regretted saying it immediately but Rosie didn't seem to hear whilst gazing at her beau. "So, where on earth is Christopher?"

"Oh, he fell hook, line and sinker for the archaeologist on the trip I organised for him in Malaga," explained Rosie. "When we came back, he started studying archaeology, just to impress the guide, and became even more boring than before. Despite all his complaints about the aeroplane, the heat, the food and the weird lift system, he's gone back to Malaga to live, so it worked out perfectly. Ironic, isn't it? Now he and Pedro the archaeologist are living together in a small flat over a bar on the outskirts of Madrid. They've set up a rescue home for unwanted handbag dogs and, despite all the risks, they're promoting gay rights all over Spain against the Social Danger Law. It's amazing that our married managed to survive for thirty years, but there were some good bits. There must have been, but my memory is not as good as it was once. I'm very happy now and don't want anything to change."

She put her arm through Alejandro's arm and gave him a happy squeeze.

"Christopher, hey? Who would have thought it?" Veronica replied in disbelief.

Veronica struggled to understand how anyone could be with someone for thirty years and not have an inkling. From the time she had spent with her in Malaga, she realised Rosie was one very smart lady. If somebody as bright as Rosie hadn't realised Christopher was gay, then she herself wouldn't have a chance if it happened to her in a relationship.

Rosie had become thoughtful and quiet so, to get back to the matter in-hand and lighten the mood between them all, Veronica chipped in, "You know Christopher needs to be careful following a career in archaeology, don't you?"

Eyes wide open now, Rosie looked up. "Why?"

"Because, Rosie, many archaeologists end up bankrupt. Did you know that?"

"Do they? Goodness me. I didn't know that. Why is that?"

"Because their career is in ruins."

Three of them laughed and eventually, when the comment was explained, Alejandro laughed too.

Tea and amazing homemade cakes were brought into the lounge and the conversation ranged around the flight to and from Malaga, and Veronica's antics on the Spanish holiday.

After the giggles had died down, Veronica eventually broached the subject she had intended to broach all along. She asked Rosie if she still had her camper van.

"Well, yes, but we don't use it much and are thinking of selling it. Why, do you want to buy it?" she asked.

Veronica suggested she and Rosie go into another room while Alejandro and Godfrey became better acquainted and tucked into Alejandro's cakes.

Veronica explained her plight. "Well, it's like this. I need to get to northern Spain with a package, which I think was stolen from a family or a synagogue during the war in...well, I actually don't know when it was stolen. In fact, neither do I know where it was stolen."

"I won't have anything to do with drugs, guns, prostitutes or slaves," Rosie said flatly.

"Nor me. I hate drugs and guns, but not as much as I hate the other two. No, they are Jewish artefacts, we think, and if we don't find the owner they'll go to auction in London and be sold to some rich guy who will probably keep them in a cupboard forever. We need to find the real owner. Will you help us?"

"How?"

"Drive Godfrey and me to Santander in northern Spain and help us locate the owner of the artefacts?"

"When?"

"Tomorrow."

"You're joking, Veronica! Tomorrow's really soon. It's nearly now!"

"No, I'm not joking. And by the way, Godfrey doesn't have any papers so he'll have to hide in your camper van toilet until we get through passport control, on the way there and on the way back."

"I need to talk to Alejandro. Give me a minute." Rosie rose to leave the room.

Before she left, Veronica asked the question, "By the way - you and Alejandro. You two OK?"

"He's a lovely, kind and very thoughtful man, the sex is

amazing, and he cooks fabulous food, too. What more could a girl want? Life for me has become wonderful. I want for nothing and live every day to the limit. For the first time in my life I'm really happy. Yes, really happy."

"I'm so pleased for you. Christopher really was a bit of an arse, wasn't he?"

Rosie laughed and left the room.

Returning five minutes later, she said, "All Alejandro wanted to know was what else were we planning to do that could possibly be more exciting, or more important, than helping two friends in need?"

A little while later, after some research into ferry times, Rosie announced, "We need to catch the ferry to Santander at 7.00 am tomorrow, and then drive wherever we're going. Our lives will be spiced up even more with a bit of mystery and intrigue, won't they?"

She sidled up to Alejandro with a twinkle in her eye. "Be here at 1.00 am tomorrow morning. We'll have the camper van ready to go."

"You're a gem, Rosie."

"I still owe you big time for Spain."

27

True to her word, Rosie's camper van was ready at 1.00 am. Godfrey and Veronica scrambled into the small back seats. Rosie sat in the passenger seat alongside Alejandro, who had opted to drive to Plymouth, two hundred and four miles away.

The four hour journey passed by event free. However, as they neared Plymouth anxieties became obvious, despite Godfrey reassuring them that things would be OK for he had loads of experience crossing borders undetected.

Alejandro added to the conversation, saying that when he was younger he had many brushes with the police. It was Veronica who reminded them that border police techniques had advanced considerably since then.

To lighten the mood, Godfrey recounted the tale about his brother, Gordon, getting into trouble with his passport about five years ago when travelling to France. "When he arrived at Paris' airport he was uncharacteristically fumbling for his passport in his bag after a particularly bumpy flight, when the irate French passport control officer asked him if he had been to France before. He said, yes. 'Then you should know, Sir, to have your passport ready,' the officer had snapped at him. Gordon apparently replied to the officer that the last time he came to France he hadn't needed one. The passport control officer had barked, 'Impossible'. Gordon, not one to beat about the bush, explained it had been in 1944, D-Day, and he couldn't find a f***ing Frenchman anywhere to give his passport to!"

The four burst out laughing.

"Apparently," Godfrey continued, "Gordon was detained for hours for using abusive language, insulting behaviour towards French officials, and I can't remember the other charges. He was also in trouble in Australia when he was asked at passport control if he had a criminal record. He said he was sorry but didn't realise it was still a requirement."

The stories broke the tension.

They were soon at passport control and rather than get into the most obvious place to hide, Godfrey climbed up into the low bedroom space above the driver and crouched right at the back. Pillows, blankets and boxes were piled in front of him and strapped down.

An officer was inspecting every camper van so Rosie jumped up and opened the door for him. He went straight for the tiny toilet and seeing it to be empty apart from brooms and cleaning equipment, wished them a pleasant onward journey and waved them through.

Alejandro drove them onto the ferry, over the bumpy joints between the quayside and the ship, and joined the line of camper vans all heading for Spain.

The four of them enjoyed the long crossing, none more than Godfrey who hadn't felt as much freedom for years, having been confined to either the funeral parlour or the care home. The crossing was one of those wonderful times when the sea was as calm as a millpond, the breeze refreshing, and the sea air cleared their heads and lungs.

Alejandro felt he was going home despite it being to a different part of Spain, and when he saw the coastline there were tears in his eyes. He missed the warmth of his motherland sun. Now he was living in cold, wet England for one reason only - to be with his Rosie. But, if she was an Eskimo, he would gladly live in an igloo just to be with her.

Rosie was about to revisit the country which had lit the blue touch paper of her lacklustre life, a country where she had enjoyed the best sexual encounter of her entire life. They both stared at the first site of land, in their own worlds.

Disembarkation went smoothly and soon they were on the road to Santander. For many hours on the trip, Veronica and Godfrey had inspected the bus tickets in the bottom of the box of artefacts, turning them over and over, but try as they might, after nearly forty years, the town of origin was too blurred to read.

As their first call was to the printed destination on the ticket, Santander, the bus station seemed like a good place to try to decipher the name of the blurred town.

At the bus station's bustling information desk, nobody appeared above ten years of age. Even with Alejandro speaking Spanish there was an unwillingness to spend much time trying to help. The noisy, long, impatient queue behind them made sure of that.

Together they left the information desk and went to

examine the arrivals board. That was of no help either as there was nothing on the board that even vaguely resembled the worn name on the tickets.

Then Godfrey had an idea. Close to the bus station was the Museum of Transport. Off they went.

Luckily, the curator had worked all his life on the buses around Santander, and it was there they discovered the name of the town they were searching for. The name of the town on the ticket was Muriedas, a small town about twelve kilometres from Santander.

With a sigh, the curator told them the bus route had been discontinued about thirty years previously in one of the big reorganisations, of which he had seen many. He did not know much about the town but believed there had been a small synagogue there once.

The twelve kilometres passed quickly with the passengers high on anticipation. As they drove slowly along the cobbled streets of Muriedas the cups and plates rattled in the cupboards of the camper van.

The streets were narrow, with the first floors of the houses leaning way past the fronts of the ground floor, and full washing lines tied the upstairs of the two sides of the streets together.

Soon, the four of them scanned, what appeared to be, a deserted town centre.

Just off the square, shaded in olive trees, they eventually found the remains of a synagogue. It was in a most dilapidated state, with bushes actually growing inside the main part. What remained of the pews were upturned and the walls were covered in graffiti. Not anti-Semitic graffiti, just the graffiti of a derelict building.

The excitement and anticipation of the four was fading fast, probably due to a mix of tiredness and disappointment. They sat quietly on a wooden seat, under the shade of ancient olive trees, in the enclosed square of a strangely empty town in northern Spain. This adventure was not going the way they intended.

Not quite as exhausted and dejected as his three passengers, Alejandro started to make enquiries at all the houses nearby but there wasn't anyone who knew anything. There was much shrugging of shoulders and calling back inside the houses to wives and husbands for help, but nothing was forthcoming.

A local priest on his way to mass eventually helped. He told Alejandro there had not been a congregation in the synagogue for thirty years or more. The only person who might be able to help them was an old Jewish man and his wife who lived way outside the town.

The camper van burst into life again and the four were soon onto the next part of their quest, their expectation now moderated by reality.

After several small olive groves and two wrong turnings, a little house came into view. Alejandro wouldn't take the camper van along the winding, potholed drive so the group decided to walk the remaining two hundred yards.

One hundred yards before they reached the cottage, they stopped to admire the setting. It stood in front of a wonderful backdrop of mountains, all covered in scrub and pine trees. The cottage, complete with its terracotta tiled roof and whitewashed walls, was guarded by a parade of chickens and ducks who loudly announced the group's arrival.

An elderly but sprightly man, sporting a kipper, a white shirt done up to the neck, black trousers, and a black waistcoat, popped out of the front door.

Delighted to have visitors, he immediately ushered them all inside his little house. His homely wife, completely dressed in black, immediately made them all tea and insisted they sit at the table, despite their protestations; true Jewish hospitality.

Inside the house it was cool and quite dark due to the small windows, but once their eyes became accustomed to the dim light, the four were amazed that everything was so clean and tidy. There was not a speck of dust anywhere, and all the brasses shone.

Veronica surmised they had lived there happily for many years. She also assumed they would end their days there, happy and together in their idyllic world. She thought their needs would be small and their fare frugal, sharing everything.

The smell of wood smoke drifted from a tiny fire smouldering in the kitchen hearth, and the stomach rumbling smell of unleavened bread lingered.

Veronica believed this lovely, old couple had everything they needed. She decided this was the way she wanted to end her days; with someone she loved very much, in a warm climate, in a house covered in mauve bougainvillea, watching sunsets. Maybe drinking a little local gin.

The old man was bright and his movements were quick when he spoke. He insisted on arranging benches from outside for all to sit around the tiny table. Visitors were a treat for the pair and he chatted with them, wanting to know where they were all from.

He slipped in and out of Spanish for Alejandro. He wanted to know how English people coped with all the rain, how could they possibly exist without making their own wine, and did everyone wear flared trousers and ride scooters?

He laughed about Englishmen drinking warm beer and the young women wearing ridiculous bouffant hair styles. He was most intrigued to know how a country as great as England could possibly have a woman as head of a political party.

This was a comment that smarted on both Veronica and Rosie, but politeness won the day.

The old man also congratulated them on their first ascent to the summit of Everest with Douglas Scott and Dougal Haston, as though the group were totally responsible for the country's politics and explorers.

Once the old, Jewish man had exhausted all his questions, Godfrey explained they were looking for the true owner of a pair of Torah Finial Bells.

The old man smiled and sighed, "Ahh, you and most of America, my friends."

His English was certainly good enough to understand their quest and his demeanour changed slightly. "There are so many fakes in the world today," he resignedly told them. "They are everywhere. Once life was all about need but now life is all about greed."

Joanne immediately sprung into Veronica's mind and she imagined her being really impatient with the old man, wanting to know immediately if the bells were real or a fake. If fake, she would have no more interest and would want to leave instantly.

The thought of Joanne, back home, discovering that the bells had gone sent a shudder down Veronica's back.

"In the old days," the old man continued, "my wife and I travelled on foot from Hungary to escape the Nazis final solution. When we left we were laughed at by many people and both our families. Why, they asked us, would we want to go to Spain where no Jews had been allowed to live openly for the last four centuries? Shortly afterwards we heard they were all dead." He shook his head sadly.

"But with forged papers and dubious Spanish ancestors we did it. The journey was hard but we did it. Then we both worked to live and to eat, to laugh and to celebrate, to have children and bring them up in the true Jewish way. In turn, we watched our children grow into fine adults and have their own children. Life was simple and life was good to us in those days. But we didn't know how lucky we were. If we'd known then what chaos was coming, we would have headed west to England or America, somewhere where we would have been safe. Then life changed completely. If you like, I'll tell you what happened during the bad years and what led to there being so many fakes?"

The four were spellbound as he went on to say, between sipping his tea, that when the soldiers started to steal works of art from the churches and synagogues during the war, the Jewish Supreme Council instructed all the rabbis in the area to have fake artefacts made, and to hide the real ones until after the war. Then, if the fakes were stolen, it wouldn't matter and the real ones could be restored to their rightful positions in places of worship after the war.

The old man went on to add, “Immediately, I set about the task as instructed by the rabbi of the synagogue in Santander because I had been a silversmith by trade before the troubles. The originals were beautifully made of gold but I, and several silversmiths like me, made replicas out of brass.”

He shrugged a Jewish shrug. “It didn’t matter what we did, they stole them all anyway - the fakes and the real ones,” he said, sighing.

Godfrey asked the old man if he would like to see the bells he had brought and was surprised by his answer.

“No, thank you. I have seen so many fakes. Are they wrapped in sheepskin? Are they in a wooden box lined with lead like so many other fakes?” he demonstrated the size of the box with his veined hands.

A very surprised Godfrey nodded but pressed the old man to look because they had come such a long way.

“Oh, very well then, just to please you.”

Alejandro walked back to the camper van and a few minutes later returned, carrying the heavy box into the tiny house.

“Before I look, please tell me how you came to have the bells.”

Godfrey explained that his brother, who had recently died, left them in a safe back in England. When the safe was eventually opened nobody knew anything about the bells. Now he and Veronica wanted to return them to their rightful owner or owners.

The old man asked Godfrey to take off the lid then passed

him a small knife. He asked him to peel back the lead on the inside of the lid, in the right hand corner.

He explained, "Each of us who were making the fakes had a mark. A mark so that we couldn't be identified and then tortured to tell where the real bells were, but secretly we could each tell who had made each set of fakes. For me, it would just be interesting to know if I could recognise the mark of the man who made these fakes after all these years."

Godfrey did as he was instructed and, sure enough, there was a mark, just as the old man said. It was the mark of a Celtic cross.

Before he showed it to the old man, he asked what his personal mark had been. The old man smiled and said a friend of his had once journeyed to Wales to visit a cousin, and when he returned he never stopped talking about such a wonderful country. The people were the friendliest he had ever met and the countryside was always green.

Another of his memories was of a cross that stood on the edge of the village green. It commemorated those local soldiers from the village who had fallen. It was a Celtic cross.

Godfrey slowly moved his hand, uncovering the mark. In fact, carved into the lid of the box were two small Celtic crosses. The room fell eerily silent.

Tears started to well up in the old man's eyes when he saw his own mark, and his shaking, bony fingers carefully traced over the carvings.

Veronica decided he must have been transported back to those desperate days, when synagogues hid their treasures, gunfire shattered the peace around their towns, and tank tracks squealed and screeched on their normally peaceful, cobbled streets. A time when every Jewish home must have lived in fear of the soldiers banging on their doors, day and night. A time when mothers and fathers lost sons, wives lost husbands, and children lost their fathers of all nationalities. A time when everyone prayed for peace and an end to the carnage.

His misty eyes cleared as he returned from those dark days to the present. His trembling hands gently unfolded the sheepskins and he carefully placed the bells on the wooden table side by side.

Despite not speaking English his wife understood what was happening and placed her old, arthritic hands affectionately on his shoulders.

He was unable to speak for a while then said, "I made these for the rabbi in Santander but they were stolen several months later by the soldiers. They must have been hidden in a stash somewhere near Santander."

He went on, "They could have remained there undiscovered for thirty years. It's more likely that when the troubles were over, some of the soldiers who were stationed here returned to the stashes and loaded lorries to transport the artefacts to various black markets across Europe. Often the locals had beaten them to it. I can only assume your brother must have bought the bells in London where many priceless oil paintings and ancient artefacts were sold privately. These fakes have only a historic interest value now. Other Jewish artefacts found their way to America, and one genuine pair of gold bells in particular has been the subject of a huge court case where their value is said to exceed twelve million dollars. The court case has gone on and on for many, many years."

He gazed back at the bells.

"Each bell took me about a month to make, working day and night. I was very proud when they were finished. Making one is easy, making two is easy, but making them identical? Now, that's where the time goes. Four months it took me. Once they were complete, I took them to the Santander rabbi who congratulated me and said he couldn't tell the difference from the real ones. I had to take them to him one at a time in a wicker basket covered in vegetables, on a crowded bus, to avoid being discovered. Finally, I took him the empty box."

"So that's why there were three bus tickets. You took one bell and returned, took another bell and returned, and finally you took the box. What happened to the real bells?" asked Godfrey. "Did the rabbi hide them?"

The old man hesitated slightly, shaking his head from side to side. "Who knows, who knows? Soon after, the soldiers broke into everyone's house in this locality as they were passing through, and stole anything that wasn't nailed down. We lost everything." He patted his wife's hand, still on his shoulder.

There was silence in the room. Nobody knew what to say about the terrible fear the old couple had experienced in the troubled times.

It was Veronica who spoke first, "Would you like to keep these bells?"

The old man looked up and said, "But they are yours, my dear."

"Would you like to keep them?" she repeated.

The old man interpreted for his wife. She put her hands to her mouth and gasped.

In the background Rosie and Alejandro were also in tears, silently watching a precious moment in life unfold. Both felt humbled but privileged to be there.

Godfrey needed a sense check and asked, "Shouldn't we check with Joanne first?"

Veronica ignored Godfrey saying, "Thank you very much for your hospitality. I hope you both enjoy these beautiful bells for the rest of your days."

The old man and his wife, both with tears in their eyes, hugged each of their unexpected but welcome visitors in turn.

As the four left the garden, and the busy chickens and noisy ducks, the old couple stood at the front door of their tiny house, hand in hand, waving them goodbye, as they made their way back to the camper van.

Veronica looked back and waved, wanting to be able to remember the scene. It seemed to her that the white walls of the couple's home were brighter, the terracotta tiles happier, and the bougainvillea mauve paper flowers more vivid.

Godfrey put his arm around Veronica and said, "That was really an amazingly selfless thing you just did. Tan would have been so proud of you, and so am I."

Veronica sniffed at the mention of Tan's name and smiled back at him.

"Where to now?" asked Rosie, breaking the mood as they clambered aboard.

"Find somewhere to eat paella, drink buckets of the local wine, sleep somewhere around here, and then head home tomorrow and decide how we're going to tell Joanne," said Veronica.

"Decide what you're going to tell Joanne, you mean," corrected Godfrey.

It had been such a momentous day, the four of them celebrated in style in a restaurant in the square in the centre of Muriedas and, as visitors were scarce, they were treated to a first-class Spanish meal.

At one stage they all stood up and toasted the old couple, hoping they would always be happy. They visualised the bells standing on the sparse mantle shelf in their little home, shining in the fire light, with the old couple holding hands and toasting the bells with glasses of homemade wine.

The next day, breakfast was a big fry up outside the camper van before they set off for Santander and home.

Once they were on the road Rosie suddenly shouted, "Stop! Alejandro, stop the van! I must have left my handbag in the old couple's house yesterday. In all the emotion I didn't miss it until now. It's got my passport, diary, purse and everything in it. We must go to the old couple's house quickly." A real anxiety showed on her face.

"No problem, no problem, my darling, we can call in the old couple's house on our way back to Santander. I'm sure it will still be there. Spanish people are all honest people," said Alejandro reassuringly, and he patted her hand.

As before, the campervan bumped to a standstill two hundred yards away from the old couple's house, and Rosie and Veronica walked up to the door. They knocked respectfully. No answer. They called. No answer.

"Oh no, this is going to be one of those occasions when they'll be driving around trying to find us to give the handbag back, and we'll be driving around looking for them," said Rosie. "This could go on for days."

"I'm sure they must have just popped out for something. Stop worrying," scolded Veronica.

They knocked a little harder and called a little louder. Veronica accidentally pushed against the front door, which wasn't locked. They peeped inside.

When their eyes became accustomed to the light, Rosie saw her handbag on the table in the middle of the room. She rushed over but it was exactly as she had left it - purse, passport, everything, just as Alejandro had said. She felt so ashamed at her first reaction that her handbag would be empty. There was real relief for both of them that the handbag was there, for without the passport there would have been endless delays to get out of the country.

The two of them looked around and soon became aware that things had completely changed. There was only the table and two chairs left downstairs.

Everything else in the house had gone: ornaments, mats, pictures, the menorah and candles, the pots and pans from the kitchen, everything. To check, they peeped upstairs and everything had gone from there too, even the two rude, built-in wardrobes were empty of their clothes, and the ancient bed had been stripped.

Outside, Rosie looked about, noticing for the first time there were no chickens or ducks to greet them. "I thought something was different when we walked towards the house, but couldn't put my finger on it. It was the lack of a welcome from the hens and the ducks."

Veronica started to laugh, and then Rosie joined in as it dawned on her what had happened.

"We've been had, haven't we?"

"Well and truly," agreed Rosie.

They sat together on the bench and Veronica worked through what had happened.

"So, the crafty old man made two sets of fakes all that time ago, that's why it took him four months to make them, not two months. I wondered why he said four months. He didn't take just one fake on each journey, he took two fakes in his basket and brought a real gold one home each visit. He left one fake and the second fake replaced a real gold one because the rabbi couldn't tell the difference. Again, on his second visit he took two fakes and returned home with the second gold one. On his last visit he took a lead box. That's the reason there were three bus tickets. When he had finished he had two real gold ones at home. He then made another lead box especially for them, but put his Celtic cross mark on it as if they were fakes, in case he was ever challenged."

Rosie took up the logic. "Then, by chance, along with all the other houses in the area, their house was robbed by soldiers who stole the real gold ones and placed them in a stash of artefacts that eventually got looted, and they ended up in London on the black market. I bet Godfrey's brother Gordon couldn't believe his luck when he was offered real gold bells.

He seems, from what you both say, the type of guy always looking for a good deal, so he stashed them away for a rainy day. Wow, some stash!"

Veronica took over again. "The old man couldn't believe his good fortune when we waltzed into his house with the real gold ones, some thirty five years later. If it hadn't been for the Muriedas bus tickets we wouldn't have known where to start. He was so convincing that they were fakes I felt really sorry for him. He and his wife must have packed up and left the moment we were out of sight in case we changed our minds, laughing all the way to who knows where? Good luck to them, I say."

"Me too," said Rosie.

Back near the camper van Rosie shouted reassuringly to Godfrey and Alejandro and waved her handbag. "It's OK, I've got my handbag. It's exactly as you said, everything is untouched. I'd left it on the table in all the emotion. Alejandro, I'm sorry I doubted you in my mind. You were right, Spanish people are honest. Let's go home."

"How were they?" asked Godfrey.

"Very, very happy," said Veronica, looking at Rosie with a smile.

"Yes, they're really very happy. Veronica did them a good turn and they'll never forget her generosity. Now, let's head back to dear old England and some rain. I do struggle with all this sunshine," Rosie joked as Alejandro gave her a hug.

28

The return journey was uneventful, despite all their anxieties.

Fortunately, a fully loaded lorry had broken down just inside the ferry boat, putting the sailing departure time from Santander in doubt. As the time rolled by with all the staff trying to move the lorry, the Spanish passport control officers and the loading team were becoming more and more agitated, working faster and faster to be off in time to catch the tide. Checks were cursory.

The crossing was rough but by the time they reached Plymouth it had calmed. Again, as per the first time, the UK passport control was relatively efficient and an officer boarded the camper van and checked the toilet. Soon they were waved on by the border police.

Once well outside Plymouth, Godfrey joined the others from his hidey-hole. The light hearted conversation about their bravery rambled around exaggerating how easy it had been to smuggle someone both ways across the border. There was a smugness in the air from the two men who didn't actually say 'I told you it would be easy', but so wanted to.

Lots of laughter followed and then it became quiet in the camper van as each of them reflected on their time together in Spain.

To pass the time on the four hour journey home, Veronica took up the mantle of telling a story. "You know I nearly didn't come on this trip after my last journey to the continent?"

"No, really?" asked Rosie.

"Yes, it was in Joanne's dad's car, towing a caravan."

"Did you have an accident?" queried Rosie.

"No, much worse! I'll tell you about it if you like," she offered. "Joanne and I were about ten years old at the time. My family, who were a bit poorer, only ever went for odd days out during the summer, so when I was offered the chance to join Joanne and her family for a two week continental holiday, I thought I was the bee's knees. She and her family went on posh holidays every year. I was so looking forward to it. I'd never been abroad before. I really liked Joanne's mum, Auntie Faith. She's still a real sport and a very special person. You'd really get on well with her Rosie. She'd help anyone, she's generous to a fault. But Joanne's dad, Uncle Tom, well, he's a bit different. He's, well, to be honest, a bit of a tosser."

Alejandro interrupted her and asked for clarification, "Tosser. What is tosser? Is this the same as in Spain, like pizza tosser?"

They all laughed.

"Well, not exactly," hesitated Veronica and, after thinking how she could explain, did a rude hand sign to denote a tosser.

Alejandro immediately joined in the laughter and said, "Oh, you mean English tosser. Now I understand."

The mood in the camper van was much lighter so Veronica continued. "Well, the night before we were due to set off the two of us were so excited her parents thought we would never go to sleep. Then Auntie Faith took a phone call. It was her mother-in-law, who Uncle Tom only tolerated for she always wanted something doing at her house, and she was a bit doddery. She was in tears at the thought of being left alone and not seeing her granddaughter for two weeks. In a rash moment, Auntie Faith suggested she come with us on holiday, to which she replied her passport was on the kitchen table and her case was already packed! Auntie Faith was a bit surprised, but as she had offered there was no going back."

She paused for breath then went on. "Then Auntie Faith had to tell Uncle Tom. Well, there was an almighty row. He blew his top, but came around in the end for Joanne was really fond of her granny. The next day, the five of us squashed into their car and set off on the long drive from Middlesbrough down to Plymouth, towing the caravan at fifty miles per hour. The journey was long and cramped, but while Joanne's granny was pulling chocolate and sweets from her bag I could put up with any discomfort," laughed Veronica.

"Well, eventually, we pulled into the Greasy Spoon transport cafe, just outside Plymouth. Joanne and I rushed to the loo because we were bursting, but Granny pulled Auntie Faith to one side and said that she had a bit of a problem. She couldn't find her passport anywhere. She must have left it on the kitchen table. After two circuits of the car park, Auntie Faith eventually brought Uncle Tom back down to earth. Joanne and I kept our distance."

"Oh my goodness!" exclaimed Rosie.

"A lengthy discussion followed where Joanne's mum and dad considered every option. Auntie Faith and Uncle Tom both decided it was too far to go back to Middlesbrough and get another ferry in three days' time. Granny couldn't go back on the train on her own, and any further delay would mean we would all miss the ferry. So, they decided to put Granny in the caravan toilet and drive through British passport control. Once on the ship they would let her out of the toilet and do the same again to go through the French passport control. Then they would drive until they were well away from the port, stop and let her out, and she would be safe enough. After the holiday they would do the same for the return journey. It reminds me of what we have just done," Veronica chuckled.

Sweets were handed round the four of them and Veronica took up the story again.

"Joanne and I were to say nothing if asked, and to let the grown-ups do all the talking. All went according to plan. Once in France, Uncle Tom drove for about thirty miles, just to be sure. In fact, there was much more room in the car with just the two of us in the back, and Uncle Tom said it was much quieter. He did ask Auntie Faith if Granny could stay in the caravan all the way to Bordeaux, but she said definitely not as they had broken enough laws for one day."

Veronica popped another sweet in her mouth and carried on.

"Eventually, Uncle Tom stopped in a lay by and Auntie Faith went back to let Granny out. She came back to the car and sat in the passenger seat ashen-faced, saying Granny was dead! There were lots of tears from all of us and Uncle Tom went to check. Sure enough, Granny was dead!"

Rosie put her hand to her mouth and said, "Oh, how terrible for you all, and you were only ten at the time?"

Veronica nodded. "After we had all stopped crying Auntie Faith and Uncle Tom decided they would leave Granny in the toilet and drive to the nearest village, find a police station and report the death. Uncle Tom drove in silence, none of us knowing what to say. Twenty miles further on, we drew up outside a police station in a remote village. 'Leave this to me. Say nothing any of you,' said Uncle Tom, because he said he did French at school. We all went inside the dusty police station..."

Veronica then recited the whole conversation between her uncle and the police sergeant who had been behind the counter verbatim, affecting accents and mannerisms.

"Pardon Monsieur, do you speak English?"

"Non."

"Oh, well here goes. Mon mere est mort."

"Eh?"

"Mon mere est tres mort."

"Eh?"

"Est tres mort dans le masion avec roues."

"Eh?"

Veronica's audience were thoroughly entertained.

"Eventually, after much impatience, the French policeman rang an English speaking colleague. He handed the phone to Uncle Tom who explained the situation, leaving out the fact that Granny was there without a passport. If they didn't ask, he wasn't going to venture that fact. The phone was passed back to the policeman whose demeanour changed when he heard the problem in French. He gestured for us all to accompany him outside to see for himself."

Veronica paused for dramatic effect.

"Outside in the street there was the car, just where we had left it, but no caravan! It had gone! We all looked up and down the street, but no caravan. It had been unhitched from our car and driven off with Granny inside. We ran up and down the street. We looked around the corners and in all the side streets in the village, but no caravan. The policeman even asked a local shopkeeper sitting outside his shop if he had seen anything, but he hadn't. We never did see the caravan again, or Granny, but the thieves who took it would have had one hell of a shock when they came to clean it," laughed Veronica.

"Oh, how terrible!" said Rosie.

Godfrey couldn't stop laughing, and neither could Alejandro.

"But that's awful," said Rosie. "I can't imagine how you must have all felt."

"Is that a true story?" asked Godfrey, as the tears rolled down his cheeks.

"It's as true as my name is Lady Veronica Sidero Puxworthy of Middlesbrough Castle."

Veronica burst out laughing at Rosie's seriousness.

Rosie cuffed Veronica's arm good humouredly and admonished her for making fun of her.

With Veronica's embellishments the story had passed at least a half hour of the journey. Traffic was light and the rest of the journey passed equally quickly.

Soon they were sitting having tea together in Rosie's lounge. Before leaving, there were big hugs and thanks, and promises to keep in touch.

Veronica's plan was to drive Godfrey back to the care home and then go on to confront Joanne about her decision to gift the bells to the Jewish couple in Spain. It was not a conversation she was looking forward to for she had seen Joanne in a rage before and knew she had a temper like a chicken... s*** and stamp in it!

Veronica could tell her that the bells were fakes. She could tell her that the old couple were the true owners of the bells. She could tell her the old couple sent their grateful thanks. She knew she could tell Joanne anything she liked but where there was money at stake, cupidity ruled.

She really wasn't looking forward to the inevitable row. Those few minutes could be terminal in their relationship. Every defensive argument had been explored by Veronica as she nervously pulled into the funeral parlour entrance.

A very anxious Vincent rushed out to meet Veronica as soon as he saw her car. He hurried her straight into Joanne's empty office and shut the door.

"What's the hurry? What's wrong?" She'd never seen the normally stoic Vincent like this before.

"Where have you been? Miss Joanne's been arrested!" blurted out Vincent.

"What? Why?"

"The police believe she's been laundering money."

"She has!"

"We know that, but they don't, or they didn't, or they weren't sure, but they are now."

"Slow down, Vincent. I don't understand. How did she get caught? She's so careful about everything."

"It happened when you were away. We were all ready to take a delivery, but what we didn't know was that close by in the neighbourhood some kids had stolen a posh car and were being chased by two police Zephyr cars and a couple of noddy bikes. This was all happening at exactly the time the delivery hearse was lining up to reverse into our garage. The kids in the stolen car smoked into our cul-de-sac on two wheels, burning rubber all the way, unaware there was no way out."

"And?" asked Veronica, sitting down to steady her legs.

"When they saw the way would soon be blocked by the hearse, the kids accelerated to get between the hearse and the wall. Unfortunately, they didn't make it. They smashed into the side of the hearse and our wall. Five seconds later and the hearse would have been in our garage, the kids would have sped past and been caught at the end of the cul-de-sac, and nobody would have been any the wiser."

He paused to draw breath before continuing.

"Before the kids could recover from the crash, the two

Zephyr police cars pulled up behind their smashed car and blocked it in. Suddenly, there were coppers everywhere. Apparently, these lads were serial car thieves, from out of town, stealing to order. The police had been waiting for them for some time and weren't going to let them get away at any price. Then it all went pear-shaped."

"How?" asked Veronica, eager to know.

"The two gorillas jumped out of the delivery hearse and rather than blag their way out of it, stupidly made the situation very suspicious for us by legging it. Who turned up but that big police sergeant who came here once before? He had a field day lording it about and once they had arrested the two lads, the big sergeant turned his attention on us. I was made to take the lid off the casket and, sure enough, it was a bandaged mummy full of money. He impounded everything and arrested Joanne. They have also been at my house to search for cash, but didn't find any."

"Didn't find any? I thought your house was like the Bank of England with all the cash you and Elsie had stashed in all the drawers, flower pots and clocks?"

"It was, but over the last month Elsie and I realised the cash was doing no good for anyone, and neither would it, so we've been sending anonymous shoe box parcels of about £20,000 to various charities, from different post offices all over the neighbourhood. The very last package went a fortnight ago. That was a huge bit of luck for us. During the house search that big police sergeant kept going up to Elsie and peering closely at her saying 'I'm sure we've met somewhere.' He only stopped when Elsie said very loudly, so that all the other police officers in the house could hear, that she had a little cleaning job at Bottoms Up, the local gentleman's strip club come brothel, and perhaps that's where he'd seen her. He stayed well away from her after that."

"And what about Joanne?" asked Veronica, her head spinning.

"Oh, it gets worse for Miss Joanne. If that wasn't bad enough, yesterday, while Joanne was still in the police station, she saw a front page article in the local paper about her five derelict houses on the promenade. Those were the ones she inherited from Gordon with compulsory purchase orders served on them. The article was celebrating that the last part of the jigsaw was now in place, with the purchase of the final five derelict houses, and the long-awaited promenade redevelopment scheme could commence. Gordon's ex saw the report and disputed Joanne's ownership, because Gordon hadn't disclosed the properties during their divorce proceedings. A court holding order was put on all Joanne's finances this morning."

"Vincent, are you or Elsie implicated in any way?" asked Veronica, getting up to make him a cup of tea to settle him down.

"No. Elsie is very upset but we both knew the risks. The total police focus seems to be on Miss Joanne."

"Am I connected in any way, or Godfrey?" asked Veronica.

"I don't think so."

"Well, thank goodness for that! And I thought I'd be pleased to be home. Oh, I forgot, what about all the coins in the big fridge? Did the police search there?"

"Yes, with a fine-tooth comb. But in Joanne's big clean up exercise she made me put all the money from folk who were still paying into the club into the bank. All the old, loose coins, and old envelopes, were shovelled into big boxes and I took them up to your dad's house. He wasn't too happy at first, but between us we managed to squeeze them all into his shed and his garage. I had to make three journeys in the hearse. He'll be busy for years to come. So, the big fridge was completely empty when the police searched it."

"Thank the lord for that. What about Humphrey?"

"Elsie took him home yesterday. He's a bit grumpy, but we'll look after him for a while."

"He's always grumpy. Talking about grumpy, I'd better go and see Joanne first thing in the morning."

"Elsie and I really don't know what to do now. Shall we just continue to run the funeral parlour as if nothing's happened?" asked Vincent nervously.

"Yes, exactly that. Do nothing out of the ordinary. Act as if nothing has happened when dealing with the clients. Don't talk to the press at any price, and both of you stay calm." Veronica instructed.

The next morning, at the police station, a conciliatory, wet-eyed Joanne was very pleased to see Veronica and gave her a long hug. She had given up her passport to the police, been in CID interviews most of the previous day, and was about to meet with her solicitor again. His expectancy was that, due to the seriousness of the crimes, she would probably be kept in custody overnight again and face at least a three year sentence.

Veronica decided Joanne could manage without the knowledge of a possible fortune having been given away in Spain at that moment.

Veronica hugged Joanne back and told her she was sure

everything would turn out all right in the end, and if things were not all right then it wasn't the end! "Come over to the care home as soon as you can. Godfrey and I will do everything we can to help you."

Veronica recounted some of the conversation she had with Vincent. She explained she had told him to continue to run things as if nothing had happened, and on no account to talk to the press. Veronica even gave Joanne an update on Humphrey. After an hour she reluctantly left a tearful Joanne.

Back at the care home, Veronica recounted Joanne's story to Godfrey who sat in silence shaking his head.

Finally, he spoke. "Isn't it a good job we moved the bells back to Spain where they belong? At least they're safe, even though they were just fakes."

Veronica coughed into her gin.

EPILOGUE

Shortly after returning from Spain, Rosie and Alejandro were married and living very happily together. They made regular trips back and forth to Spain in their camper van, which they had decided to keep, and although their trips weren't quite as exciting as the trip they took with Veronica and Godfrey, they thoroughly enjoyed them.

Rosie appeared to look younger every time Veronica saw her; she was even more alive and full of life and sparkle. There was a happy glow about the couple whenever they were together. Rosie said it was Alejandro's cooking but Veronica knew differently. No amount of pasta or paella could make her eyes that bright.

Six months later, Veronica felt she had to make some changes to the smooth running of Bethesda Care Home and offered Rosie the vacant position of domestic services manager.

It was a very good decision, for within weeks of Rosie's arrival the whole home positively shone. Rooms were brighter, the linen crisper and whiter, and all the woodwork was polished to a high shine.

At the same time, Alejandro was offered the job of head chef at the home, and his creative, culinary flair transformed the food at breakfast, lunch and dinner time.

Nine months on, Vincent completely retired when the new owners bought the funeral parlour. Veronica offered him the job of driving her about until she finally managed to get around to taking her driving test. Occasionally, she complained bitterly about his driving, for he had retained the habit of travelling at cortege speed.

At exactly the same time that Vincent retired, Elsie kicked off her white abattoir wellies, hung up her long, red, rubber apron and rubber gloves for the very last time, and set up her dream business.

She'd always wanted to run her own sandwich van company called Lettuce Feed You, delivering top of the range sandwiches to office blocks in the town at lunch time.

The rest of the day she helped to look after one of their chosen charities for children. Vincent and Elsie also helped in the gardens at Bethesda during the busy seasons of summer and autumn.

And Humphrey? Well, he settled into life with Vincent and Elsie and was still as grumpy as ever, coughing up fur balls and having flatulence after preening his nether regions.

Following legal advice twelve months on, Godfrey decided to confess to the authorities that he had been stateless since the war, but offered to pay back everything he owed in National Insurance and Income Tax to the government.

This was not enough for the court so, as he was waiting to

be sentenced, Veronica took up his case and informed the Army of his plight. When his regiment heard he was still alive they were all over him, wanting to tell his story to the world and announcing in the local and national papers that Godfrey was a hero. He became the only deceased soldier in the history of the British Army to accept his own medals.

The Army PR team wanted to do a big feature on him for his bravery. As a result, in view of all the publicity, the court could do little else and gave him a suspended sentence.

Godfrey took up the full time position of head gardener in charge of the extensive Bethesda Care Home gardens. It was an outside job and he was in heaven.

Joanne only served eighteen months of her three year prison sentence and was released for good behaviour. Veronica was speechless!

However, Joanne lost the battle for the promenade properties to Gordon's ex-wife, and the Compulsory Purchase Order money was recovered by the court because the properties had not been disclosed in Gordon's divorce settlement.

The funeral parlour was seen by the court as ill-gotten gains and the proceeds of crime, and confiscated along with any money Joanne had saved.

Whilst in prison, Joanne had been struck off all the professional accounting bodies to which she belonged, prohibiting her from practicing as an accountant in the future.

On her release, and having studied for a care assistant's qualification, Veronica offered her a permanent position working as a regular night shift care assistant at the

Bethesda Care Home. She wore a Lincoln green uniform, had a proper contract, an upside down watch, and was aiming for her full nursing qualifications.

As a surprise for Joanne's birthday, Veronica booked them a holiday together - two economy flights to Malaga and accommodation in the same hotel, in the same shared room, as last time.

The bathroom, once again, had pointed toilet paper and smelled of a sandalwood and pomegranate disinfectant tsunami.

They smiled at each other when they heard a stag party in full swing down in the bar area, just as noisy as the last time. Their bedroom window looked out onto an even bigger heap of crashed and broken supermarket trolleys.

They toasted each other with gin and tonic...with lots of ice!

OTHER BOOKS BY HOWARD G AWBERY

A Sprig of Mint

The Odd Noble Deed

The Music Box

Me and My Lamp

Five Strange Tales

Five Even Stranger Tales

Isobelle

Lightning Source UK Ltd.
Milton Keynes UK
UKHW010047121120
373227UK00003B/907